Welcome to LILIM

LINDA COLLIGAN

Sculptures and Sketches by Virgil Colligan

NEWMAN SPRINGS PUBLISHING
320 Broad Street
Red Bank, NJ 07701

First originally published by Newman Springs Publishing 2024

ISBN 979-8-89308-048-3 (Paperback)
ISBN 979-8-89308-049-0 (Digital)

Printed in the United States of America

To my husband, Virgil.

If you look really hard over the edge of the steep cliff, past the tree with the waving arms far below the ferns; if you look really hard, you will see the spot under the mushroom patch, which is Lilim. A dusty cave with a stream running through the middle of it. High on the cliff in the cave you will see…

Chapter 1

One beautiful fall morning, Emil had just finished breakfast and ran straight up to his room and grabbed his sword. Yesterday, it was raining, and Emil could not go outside. He was running around the house, knocking things over with his hard plastic sword, and Mom had gotten mad. Yesterday, she had made Emil put the sword away and do quieter things in the house. Today, however, the sun was shining, and Emil was allowed to play with his sword. Once again, Emil began running around the house with his sword, pretending to stab at everything and, once again, knocking things over.

"Emil!" his mother yelled. "Go outside with that sword and play. You are knocking over everything!"

Emil frowned and replied, "But…" Before Emil could blurt out a reason, his mother replied, "But nothing. Go outside and play." Emil took his sword and the shield that he had made to ward off any attackers and went outside.

It was a cool fall morning with the leaves falling. Emil used his sword. He swung and stabbed at a falling leaf as if it were his enemy. Emil continued stabbing at leaves as he walked over the hill and down toward the woods to his friend Shelly's house. She lived on the other side of the woods across the stream. They went to school together. But it was Sunday and there was no school today, only football.

Emil walked over the log—the log that he and Shelly had put there in order to cross the stream and not get their feet wet. Emil was rocking the log back and forth as he continued to stab at the leaves and things that were not there. As Emil attempted to stab at one of the falling leaves, the log rolled. Emil was trying to catch his balance, wavering back and forth on the log. He jumped off the log, falling onto the ground. Emil got up, shook himself off, and looked back at the log. It was now half in the stream. Emil, not worrying about the log, continued on his way to Shelly's house. His sword, wet from the stream, made it feel like rain as he continued to stab leaves over his head as they fell from the trees. Emil was making up stories in his mind as he continued stabbing in the air.

Meanwhile, Shelly was blaring her music on her stereo and dancing around her room. Shelly's dad called to Shelly, "Turn off that music and go outside. It's a beautiful sunny day outside. I can't hear what's going on with my Jets game with all that noise you are mak-ing." Shelly quickly shut off her music and headed directly outside.

Emil reached Shelly's house as she was walking out the door. "Hi, Emil. My dad kicked me out of the house because I was making too much noise, and he could not hear the football game," Shelly said as she saw Emil running up the path stabbing at leaves.

Emil replied, "My mom kicked me out too. Get your sword and we will go. I saw knights on horseback in the woods. I think that they have treasure with them."

Shelly responded, "You have a great imagination, but I can't get my sword, my dad will kill me if I go back inside."

Emil frowned. "What do you want to do? Oh, I got it, I will make you a spear. Come on, we will find a good stick in the woods, and I will make a spear for you. We can hunt down those knights and get their treasure." Shelly followed without saying a word, just listening to Emil's story of the knights. Shelly loved going on the adventures that Emil created in his mind.

Emil, while running his sword through the leaves, found a stick. He picked it up and threw it. *Too small*, he thought. Emil then found another stick and picked it up. Emil brushed the leaves off of the stick and peeled the bark off of the one end. "Here," he said as he handed Shelly the stick. "This is your spear. We have to start at the river because the knights broke the bridge. It's halfway in the river, and we need to fix it before it flows down river, and we have no bridge."

Emil and Shelly always pretended that the stream was a huge river. They also pretended that the log was a huge fallen tree that they put there to cross the river into another world. In this world, they would create scenarios of knights and kings and damsels in distress. Emil and Shelly would spend hours in this world playing until dark.

Once at the stream, Emil and Shelly put down their spear and sword in order to try and move the log that had fallen. As they were moving the log back into place, Emil spotted out of the corner of his eye a black bear moving slowly toward them.

"Shelly," Emil whispered. "There is a bear to my right."

Shelly slowly looked toward the bear. "Uh-*oh*. W-w-w-what should we do?" questioned Shelly.

"We need to make some noise and then slowly move away," said Emil quietly.

But as they were about to make some noise, the bear stopped moving. It looked down at its leg as if something was biting it.

"Emil," whispered Shelly, "the bear stopped moving. Let us move to the top of that hill now that the bear is not focused on us."

"Good idea," said Emil. The two slowly crossed the log that they had just gotten into place. They walked up to the top of the hill and hid behind a tree, all the while watching the bear.

The bear began to swat at its leg and grunt. It continued to grasp at its leg and grunt even louder. The bear pulled its leg away and ran into the woods in the other direction. Across the stream, and safely on a hill overlooking the stream, Emil wondered what chased the bear away. At the same time, Shelly said to Emil, "What chased the bear away?"

Emil laughed. "Ha, ha, ha, I was just thinking the exact same thing."

Shelly laughed and smiled. "We should go try to figure it out now that the bear is gone."

"Okay," said Emil and the two of them went down the hill to the stream and across the log. Once over the log, they picked up their sword and spear. They turned left and walked into the woods to where the bear had been standing. They could see claw marks on the ground where the bear had been clawing at its leg. Nothing else, only claw marks in the leaves and the dirt. The claw marks had moved some of the leaves aside. This revealed a tree stump just below the surface. Brushing away more of the leaves and dirt, Emil looked at the stump. The top of the stump showed the rings of the tree to be over one hundred years old. The rings were glistening, like the wood had been covered with preservative to ensure that it would not rot. Just below, in what was left of the bark, one could see tiny holes like needle marks.

Chapter 2

It has only come about in the past several years that the children of Lilith have come to be seen by the outside world. Somewhere near the Red Sea, at dawn, if you look hard enough over the edge of the cliff, is a cave. Look really hard and you may see a glimpse of the beings of Lilim. These are the ones that are not in your nightmares. They have taken on a new life. In their Lilim, there is peace.

After being left to fend for themselves, the children of Lilith have created their own civilization using garbage and items left behind by our civilizations to create their own way of living. The children of Lilith split up into their own cultures. They grouped themselves according to how they got along with each other. Lilith's children spread themselves out among the entire earth. Some stayed near their original home by the Red Sea, and others went to the far ends of the earth to be on their own. Each culture created its own society with its own laws and governed its own way. Although they were all children of Lilith, the ones that created Lilim were kind, peaceful, and helpful to others.

The children of Lilim were scavengers. They picked up any-thing that they could find and found a use for it. Lilim is underground, far below the earth. You can only get there through the roots of the oldest trees. These roots lead to a cave in which the children of Lilim live.

Chapter 3

"What do you think scared the bear away?" asked Shelly.

"It was us," replied Emil as he smirked.

"Ha-ha," replied Shelly. Emil seemed stumped as he stared at the stump.

"The bear was right here. And all I can see is this stump of a tree where it looked like the bear was scratching," said Emil as he put his hand on his chin and pondered the stump.

Shelly got down on her knees and took a long close look at the stump. All she could see was little pinprick holes, like the tree had been stabbed with a needle about fifty times. The wind blew leaves over the stump, and Shelly pushed them away as Emil bent down to get an even closer look. The sun gleamed through the trees, shining a ray of light onto the stump, and it glistened as if it were just polished.

Both Emil and Shelly grew tired of looking at the stump. They started to stand and stretch, and as Shelly went to take a step away from the stump, she stepped to her left and tripped. Shelly fell, bracing with her hands as she landed with a hard thump.

"Are you all right?" asked Emil as he reached out his hand to help her up. Shelly began to reply, "Yesssss…" as she grabbed the root that she had tripped on with one hand and Emil's hand with the other. Shelly couldn't move. Shelly was being pulled down by the root at the same time she was being pulled up by Emil.

"I can't move! I can't let go of the root. It won't let me go!" Shelly yelled.

Emil responded, "Try harder, I am losing my balance." And with that, Emil fell onto Shelly, and they were both dragged down by the root of the tree.

Farther and farther they went down. The root had grabbed them and transformed them into itself. They were floating down through the root, deeper and deeper into the earth. Lower and lower down the root system they went. Until finally, hand in hand, they landed softly and upright in a space that was white. It was white everywhere. There seemed to be nothing behind them, yet they could go no farther. It was as if there seemed to be some sort of wall behind them. And in front of them seemed to be an entrance to a tunnel.

Shelly and Emil looked at each other. "How did that just happen? I mean, the roots of a tree and here we stand. What is this place?" wondered Shelly.

Still holding hands, Emil looked all around, pulling Shelly in a circle to see the entire area. "I don't know. Did you hit your head? Did I hit my head? Are we dreaming?" All these questions came out of Emil's mouth but not waiting for a response. "Are you okay?" he asked Shelly.

"Yes, how about you?" she replied.

"Good, I guess." Answered Emil.

Emil let go of Shelly's hand and gestured to what looked like an entrance to a path down a tunnel. Since there was no other direction to go but forward, Shelly followed Emil to the entrance. The entrance looked small, but as they approached, it grew so that they could fit through the tunnel.

"How is this happening?" asked Shelly.

"I don't know, but it's awesome. Weird, but intriguing. Everything that we were trying to imagine with our scenarios of the knights game that we play," responded Emil.

Shelly thought to herself, "A real adventure or a dream?"

"How could we both be dreaming the same thing?" asked Emil.

"I said that out loud. I thought that I was just thinking it," replied Shelly. They walked farther and farther down the white earthen tunnel. With each step, the tunnel lit up like there were light sensors, but there weren't any lights. It was like natural light coming from everywhere and nowhere at the same time.

As they went farther into the tunnel, the lights stayed lit, but behind them was dark. "Where do you think this leads?" asked Shelly.

"I don't know, but we are going to find out," replied Emil. Shelly's head was buzzing with a thousand and one questions, but she knew that there were no answers to them. So she didn't bother to ask them. Emil and Shelly continued down the tunnel. What seemed like hours had only been fifteen minutes.

"Look ahead, there seems to be a bigger opening. Maybe we have finally found a cave or even a way out," said Emil.

"I don't think it's a way out because we don't even know how we got here. Or where here is," replied Shelly. They slowed down as they approached the bigger opening.

Then out of nowhere appeared an evil-looking creature. It was just about as tall as Emil and Shelly were. It had an eerie withdrawn face and long fangs and dark black eyes. Its body was fat and obesely round with the legs of an elephant. It had stubs for arms. And beside the fangs were two elephant trunks, but shorter than an elephant. The creature snarled at them as it appeared. Emil grabbed Shelly's hand, and they began to run back down the long tunnel. But this time, the lights did not come on like when they walked up the tunnel. It was dark.

"Hurry!" shouted Emil as he felt himself pulling Shelly.

"I'm running as fast as I can, but I can't see in the dark, and it's getting closer," answered Shelly.

The creature, although fat and clumsy, could run, and it was gaining on Emil and Shelly. It snarled, and you could hear the *tad-thump, tad-thump* of its feet as it ran down the tunnel after them.

"It's gaining on us!" shouted Shelly. *Tad-thump, tad-thump, tad-thump, tad-thump, tad-thump*—you could hear it, and it was almost upon them. They had reached the beginning of the tunnel, and they were trapped. There was no place to run. No exit. *Tad-thump, tad-thump*, the creature was coming closer. With his eyes adjusting to the dark, Emil said, "Get behind me. I will protect you. Give me your spear."

"Here," said Shelly as she got behind Emil. Emil, with his sword in one hand and the spear in the other, stood steady. *Tad-thump, tad-thump*, the creature had arrived. And with its odorous breath of rotten eggs, it put its evil face right up to Emil's face. Its dark black eyes starred into Emil's frightened eyes. As the drool from its long fangs slithered onto Emil's face and burnt, you could hear the sizzle of Emil's skin as if it were having acid dripped on it. And the smell of burning skin made Shelly scream, "Go away! Go away! Go away!" But to no avail. Emil stood frozen.

Chapter 4

Hugo

s sure as this evil creature had appeared, another one appeared right up behind it. This one was strange looking but did not have that evil appearance. This creature had a fat body but seemed proportionate to its size. It was the size of Emil and Shelly in height. It had a long tail that seemed to be used as an extra hand. It had one long leg and one round fat leg that looked like a tree trunk that it was leaning on. It had a little arm that rested on its fat leg. It held a spear in one arm and its tail held another weapon. In its other short arm or stump, it held a shield. The shield was covered with faces that stuck out from it. This creature did not snarl or say anything. It just tapped the other elephant-like creature on the back with its spear. The elephant-like creature then turned around. *Tad-thump, tad-thump, tad-thump*. Staring with its bloodshot eyes and drooling, it snarled at the new creature. The new creature drew its spear and other weapon with its tail and pointed them both at the elephant-like creature. With a snarl, the elephant-like creature took one big leap into the air and vanished.

Shaking and frightened, Emil looked at Shelly. "Are you okay?"

Shelly took her shirt sleeve and put it up to Emil's face. "*Ouch!*" replied Emil.

"I'm okay," said Shelly, "but your face has a burn mark on it."

"I'll be okay," replied Emil. As they were talking to each other, they were also turning toward the new creature.

"Who are you?" asked Shelly.

"What was that?" asked Emil.

The new creature did not speak. It just turned around and slowly went back up the tunnel. After a few feet, it turned and looked at Emil and Shelly. The creature stood there not saying anything, just looking at them. As they began to follow, the creature again turned and slowly went down the tunnel.

As they reached the spot where the elephant creature appeared, Shelly grabbed Emil's arm. "Wait. What if another one of those elephant-like creatures appear again?"

Emil turned to Shelly "We have this new creature guide. It scared away the elephant creature. So I don't think that we will run into another one. I just wish someone, or something, would talk to us." Emil said really loud and directed it toward the creature, "And let us know where we are."

They reached the bigger opening. What they had thought to be a cave was not. It was a big, bright open space. There seemed to be nothing around, just white light coming from everywhere and nowhere.

Then again, as if from nowhere, another creature appeared. This one was skinny and smaller than the other two. This one had two long legs with a unproportionally small body and a normal size head for its appearance. It had one long arm. It's one leg was fatter at the hip and wound around its back to link to its tail.

"Welcome to Lilim," it said as a sign with the word *Lilim* appeared in its hand.

"Who are you? And where are we? And what is Lilim?" replied Emil in a shaky voice.

Without waiting for an answer, Shelly spoke shyly, "How do we get home?"

The creature with the Lilim sign answered, "All these questions, but we need to know, how did you get here? No one has ever been here before except our kind."

Now a little more relaxed, Emil began again. "Who are you? Where are we? And what is Lilim?"

Again the creature with the sign answered, "All these questions, but we need to know how did you get here?"

Shelly began. "Hi, I'm Shelly, and this is my best friend, Emil." She held out her hand but realized that the creature only had one hand and it was holding a sign. Before Shelly could put down her hand, the creature with the sign shook Shelly's hand. The sign had disappeared.

"Glad to meet you." the creature said and held out his hand to Emil. As Emil shook his hand, Shelly continued. "We were in the woods looking at a stump where the bear had been. I fell, and we were pulled down by a root."

One Arm

"Oh, dear. I didn't know that humans could go through our root system. Oh, dear I…I have to go see our leader. Stay here with Hugo," replied the creature. And with that, the creature with the sign had disappeared as quickly as he had appeared.

"I wish that these guys would stop disappearing," said Emil as he began to look around at all the whiteness. As Emil explored the whiteness, Shelly stared at Hugo. "Hugo," she began, "what did the other creature mean when he said that he didn't know that humans could go through the root system? What is the root system? Where exactly are we? And how do we get home?" No answer. Shelly stared even harder. "Don't you speak?" Hugo didn't answer. He just stood there and watched.

Soon the creature with the sign appeared again. "Welcome to Lilim," he exclaimed. "If you follow me, we can find a comfortable place to sit, and all will be explained." The creature with the sign began to walk farther into the light, but there seemed to be no end.

Shelly and Emil followed, but it seemed like they were going nowhere. Just then appeared an opening. It was a wooded area. They were in the woods again but not like at their house. They were high on a cliff. The two creatures began to go down the steep cliff.

As Emil and Shelly followed, the path seemed to be a slightly graded slope; not the steep cliff they had been on. They followed the creature with the sign and Hugo down the steep cliff, far below the ferns and past a tree with waving arms to a mushroom patch. Then there appeared a cave. It was a dusty cave with a stream running through it. The first thing that caught their eyes was high on a cliff in the cave. They could see what appeared to be a jester. It was as tall as Hugo and about as bulky. It had what looked like a jester's hat on. It had two legs that were long and bent at the knees. They didn't seem like they could hold its weight because it was sitting on the ground with one leg in front and the other leg in back. It had two stubby arms, and they were holding a pole with a string on it, like a fishing pole. Yet from the pole was a rope and a tiny creature the size of a toad was hanging from it.

Jester

Chapter 5

The cave was huge. There were all kinds of things that Emil and Shelly had seen before. The things that we use every day were converted into weapons, shields, housing, you name it. There was so much to see that Emil and Shelly just stared in awe.

The creature with the Lilim sign questioned, "Are you coming? You can see more once you have rested."

Shelly, still stunned, said, "Of course, we are coming, but what do we call you?"

"Oh, I am One Arm. We were named by our deformities or looks. We embrace who we are, what we look like, and what we can do."

Once again, Emil questioned, "Where are we?"

One Arm answered, "Lilim, I already told you that. We are in Lilim."

Again, Emil questioned, "Where is Lilim? What is Lilim? How come you all look strange, and why do you call us human?"

One Arm, a little sterner now, said, "All your questions will be answered, but first you must rest and then get some food. Then I will take you to see our leader."

They continued walking, all the time passing all different creatures, none of which they had seen in their woods. They walked until they came to a basket, or what looked like a huge round laundry basket on its side.

"Here, you can rest here," said One Arm. Emil and Shelly walked into the basket and found a place to lay down. They were very tired from all this.

As they were drifting off to sleep, Emil wondered, "How can this be? This is a laundry basket like mom's but we can stand in it."

Shelly, barely keeping her eyes open, replied, "We are not at your mom's house, and all the stuff here seems to be an odd size…"

While Emil and Shelly slept, all the creatures of Lilim came together for a meeting. No one outside of Lilith's children had ever been to Lilim before. As the crowd of creatures were all asking each other how this could be and what will they do and what will happen, a hush came over them as the leader approached.

The leader was a tall guy. He had no legs and one little arm to his right side. He was sleek, and he wore a hat like a witch's but tall and slender. In the middle of the hat, in front, poked the top of the leader's head. He had a huge nose and deep-set eyes that portrayed that he was knowledgeable. They called him Tall One, the leader.

Tall One was quiet when speaking. "This has never happened. We have never had any outsiders in Lilim. Once we discover how they got here, we will need to find a way to stop others from coming down the same way. This could cause the end of our way of life as we know it." There was dead silence. "We need to welcome our guests and figure out how they will be able to return home. And what will they tell others when they return home."

A mumble rang through the crowd of creatures. "Who went up top to help or scavenge and left a trail?" asked Tall One. Dead silence again as all of the creatures looked at one another.

Big Floppy Ears stepped forward. He was tinier than the others, the size of a small toad. He had two stout legs, one stout arm, and only a stub of another arm. He had a small head, a long tail, and big floppy ears. In the stout arm, he held a rope and a shovel that he held like a spear. In the other stub of an arm, a shield made out of a tea light candle wrapper.

Big Floppy Ears started out quietly, "I was up top like any other normal day. Looking for items to use in our village." He then began to get louder. "I had just finished my search, and in finding nothing, I was just about to come home. When all of a sudden, this huge black bear, who was standing right above me, began to grunt and it slowly moved toward the children. I did what I was taught and that was to be good and practice good. So I took my shovel and began to stab at the bottom of the bear's paw as he tried to step. But the bear froze and began to swat at its leg and grunt even louder, and the children were able to run away. Then as soon as the bear began to run away, I came home."

Everyone's eyes turned to Tall One. He looked confused for a moment and replied, "We must wait until the children awake, and then they will be questioned, and we will decide how to proceed. Until then, go about your business. Big Floppy Ears, you will see to the children, and when they awake bring them to me."

"Yes," replied Big Floppy Ears.

Tall One

Chapter 6

Big Floppy Ears

ig Floppy Ears went to the basket house to see if the children had awoken. Emil was just rolling over and seemed startled by Big Floppy Ears. However, he was startled because he thought that everything was a dream.

Emil looked over and saw Shelly. "Are you awake?" whispered Emil.

Shelly was awake and had been for a while, but she had pretended to be asleep because she didn't know what to think. "Yes, I've been awake for a while, but I'm scared and confused. I thought that I had some weird dream and then I woke to this."

Emil rolled over onto his elbow and faced Shelly. "We have another guest."

"Are you two all right?" questioned Big Floppy Ears. He continued without letting them answer "I am Big Floppy Ears."

"That's so cute," replied Shelly before Big Floppy Ears could continue.

Big Floppy Ears stood with a stern look. "It's not supposed to be cute. As I was saying, welcome to Lilim. Did you rest well? Can I get you anything before we go and see Tall One?"

Emil and Shelly were now standing and stretching. "We are fine. Who is Tall One?" replied Emil.

"I didn't mean to offend you," answered Shelly.

"We will go see Tall One, who is our leader, and have something to eat and figure out how you got to Lilim. Follow me," said Big Floppy Ears as he started to walk. Emil and Shelly followed Big Floppy Ears out of the basket house. Now awake and rested, they stopped and took in the vastness of the cave. To their right was two crates, one on top of the other used as housing of some sort. Beyond that and below them was a stream. There were a few porcupine quills on either side of the stream, jutting out of the earth. Beyond the stream were other basket-type buildings. To their left and across the bridge, which was actually a floor grate, was Hugo's Café.

They didn't have to go far to get to the café. Out of the basket and across the grate stood Hugo, cooking over a barbeque. Near the barbeque were tables and chairs. Big Floppy Ears seated the two children. "Tall One will be with you shortly. In the meantime, Hugo will get you something to eat."

Hugo brought Emil and Shelly what looked like a hamburger. Shelly and Emil looked at each other puzzled. Hugo questioned, "Aren't you hungry?"

Still puzzled by what was in front of him, Emil replied, "Yes. But what is this? It looks like a hamburger, but with all this weird stuff, I just don't know."

As Emil was talking, Shelly took a bite. When Emil finished and before Hugo could get a word in, Shelly replied, "Emil, it's good. It tastes like a hamburger. Don't be rude. Sorry for Emil's rudeness. Thanks for the meal. Emil just eat."

Hugo replied, "You are welcome, and I hope that you enjoy it." Hugo walked back to the grill. With his mouth full of food, Emil replied, "I was just kidding." Shelly and Emil finished their meal in silence, all while looking around at all the odd things and creatures in Lilim.

Tall One approached the two children and greeted them, "Welcome to Lilim. I hope you are rested. I am Tall One. Did Hugo feed you?"

"Yes," replied Emil.

"Good," said Tall One. "Then we can get started. I know that this all seems a bit confusing, so we will take it slow. Before I answer your questions, I need to know how you got to Lilim."

Emil and Shelly looked at each other. "I will begin," said Emil. "We were playing in the woods, as we do all the time, near our home. Then I saw a big black bear. It was coming toward us. As we were about to try and scare it, the bear began swatting at its leg. So we took advantage of that and went to the top of the hill and watched. Then the bear ran away."

Big Floppy Ears chimed in, "Just as I said, I poked the bear's leg with my shovel, and it ran away. I then went down the root system as I always do."

"Everything sounds okay," said Tall One. "But I still do not know how you got to Lilim."

"I will continue," stated Shelly. "Once the bear was gone, we, Emil and I, decided to see what had scared the bear. All we found was an old tree stump. It glistened in the sunshine. There were little holes on the side of the trunk near the ground where there was no bark. The holes were tiny like little pinpricks. I got down on the ground and looked closer. But could find nothing. As I got up, I tripped on the root. As Emil tried to help me up, I grabbed the root with my other hand for support to get up. But the root would not let go."

Emil then began, "I pulled hard, but the root pulled us down into the ground. We somehow ended up in the root and began falling until we reached bottom. We started down the tunnel and found an opening. But then this creature, the one that looked like an elephant—"

Before Emil could finish, Tall One began "We must secure our borders. Hugo let everyone know to be on high alert for our Fallen Brothers. Go on."

Emil questioned, "Okay, who was the elephant creature? Who are our Fallen Brothers? Where is Lilim? How do we get home? And what exactly is this place?"

"Slow down, slow down. All your questions will be answered, but we still are not sure how you got pulled down into the root system," responded Tall One.

"Big Floppy Ears," called Tall One.

"Yes," answered Big Floppy Ears.

"Did anything follow you down through the root system?"

"No," he replied.

"What about Elephant Man? Did you see him when you got near Lilim?" asked Tall One.

"No," he replied again.

"Hugo," called Tall One. "How did you know that Elephant Man was near Lilim?"

Hugo responded, "I smelled him. I smelled Elephant Man, so I ventured out to see why he was lurking around. What I found was these two children cornered by Elephant Man, and he was hurting Emil with his foul drool. So I did what I always do, I made my presence known, and he left. It was odd though. I could smell the foul drool coming from the root system near our exit to Lilim. So he must have been in the root system."

Tall One replied, "We must gather a team together to go and see if our Fallen Brothers have been pulling people down the root system! If they have, then we must decide what to do about this and how to deal with our Fallen Brothers. And see if we can determine how long this has been going on. Also, see if this is the first time within our realm. Go Hugo and gather a team together and bring them to me."

Hugo leaves to gather the proper creatures to respond to Tall One's quest. Hugo chooses to lead the quest. He then opts for Rooty who helped develop the root system in which they travel.

Rooty looks like a root that opens like a flower at one end. This is his face, which has a bold nose and two deep, beady eyes. He has two arms. The left arm is longer than the right. This helps him to lead the roots into each other, in order to form the root system.

Next, Hugo chooses Mush because he can sneak anywhere and see what is going on without being noticed. Mush looks like a blob of green, blue, and purple color with a red beard. He has a mushy face with slashes for his eyes, nose, and mouth. He has one back leg on the left and one tiny arm on the right.

Finally, Hugo picks Snailstein, who can solve any dilemma brought to him. Snailstein is distinguished looking. He has two green arms like tentacles that he folds over his white oblong belly. He wears a blue cape with white polka dots. The cape has a ruffle that lays over the back of the cape. The top of the ruffle is pink and below the pink is light orange and dark orange, which alternate in triangles. In front is a green and white striped turtleneck, which he wears to cover his white body. He has a tiny round green head with two little ears on the top of his head. He has no feet and hovers about.

The group of creatures return to Tall One. "Good," replies Tall One. "Did Hugo fill you all in, and do you all know what is expected of you on this quest?"

"Yes," they all chimed at once.

"Then on your way," responded Tall One.

As they left, Tall One turned to Emil and Shelly. "We will get some drinks, go down to the river, sit, and I will tell the tale of Lilim."

Big Floppy Ears gather the children of Lilim to meet at the river.

Rooty

Snailstein

Chapter 7

Mush

Tall One began his tale of Lilim. It all started a long, long time ago. Before Eve, there was Lilith (our mother); she cheated on Adam with all kinds of evil. After finding out, Adam banished Lilith from Eden. So Lilith left to create a place of her own. Her legendary children were created from the evil of the world. They were part animal (demon) and part human. Thus, creating the creatures that envelop your nightmares. The legend says that Lilith is said to have spawned one hundred children a day.

We scattered to all ends of the earth. Going underground so as not to be seen until the right time. Lilith's children were born from evil, and so they learned to be evil. Some enter your room at night from under your bed, some through your closet, and even some through the tiniest crack in your attic. They get into your thoughts and become part of your dreams (nightmares) and sometimes even your daydreams. They stay hidden from sight because they can morph to any shape that they need to be to become what they want until the right time in order to show their power.

Evil is what was unleashed on the earth from the earliest of times. It was not until about seven hundred years ago when our generation of children were born that things began to change. The children of Lilith were not all evil. So we, the creatures of Lilim, ventured out on our own to create a place where we could live and not have to be tortured by our evil brothers. We created Lilim; a peaceful place. We chose names for each of us to make us feel more human so to speak. We created this place away from our Fallen Brothers, as we call them. From time to time, we run into them when we are out in the world above ground. But we keep to ourselves, and if we do not interfere with their taunting, then they do not interfere with us. We teach the children of Lilim to be kind to all of God's creatures.

Just like our Fallen Brothers, we can morph into any size or shape. This is how we can go through the root system and come out the same as when we started. We only morph to use the root system or when we are in great danger. You two somehow have managed to do the same without morphing. However, your size has changed down here. If you saw us out in the world above, we would be tiny from the size of a mouse to the size just below our knee. We need to find out who got you here and how in order to get you back home. We have never brought anyone into the root system. Only items from above and those items revert to their original size. You two are our size here in Lilim. Hopefully the quest will be successful, and we will be able to get you two home. I am tired now and I must rest. I will leave you with Big Floppy Ears, and he will finish showing you two around Lilim.

Chapter 8

The four creatures, Hugo, Rooty, Mush, and Snailstein, head out through the woods of their world to find out where some of their Fallen Brothers live. Out through the mushroom patch, past the ferns, and up past the tree with the waving arms, they headed out onto another path that was in the middle of the steep cliff.

"Once we find the residents of our Fallen Brothers, Mush, you will infiltrate their colony and get any information that you can on what they have been up to," stated Hugo.

"Okay," replied Mush.

Hugo continued, "I will go with you for any support you may need. Rooty and Snailstein will continue to the root system and see who has been going through it. Also, go up top and see if you can find something live to put into the root system. See how that works. Something small."

Rooty replied, "Yes, but the root system is just comprised of roots, so I will choose something very small so as not to destroy anything within the root system."

Snailstein, with his deep, distinguished voice, replied, "We will deduce what can and cannot go through the root system. We will find out who and what has been through the root system. Where shall we join up to give you our results?"

Hugo looked at Snailstein's beady eyes. "We will join up at my café and grill to discuss our results with Tall One and see what steps to take next."

As they walked through the woods, they looked for any signs of their Fallen Brothers. They neared the entrance to the big lighted area.

"Shall we go farther into the woods or split up here?" asked Rooty.

"Hush," replied Hugo. "Look ahead toward the fallen tree. There is something that I have not seen there before."

"What is it?" asked Mush.

Snailstein replied in his deep, distinguished voice, "It looks as if our Fallen Brothers have been in the woods and may live nearby. It looks like fused glass, which I believe only Elephant Man's foul drool could create."

Hugo looked at his fellow creatures. "We will split up here. I believe that our Fallen Brother's lair maybe close, and we do not want to waste any time." Rooty and Snailstein head toward the root system.

Hugo, along with Mush, went forward to investigate the fused glass. As they approached the fallen tree, Hugo states, "Smell that awful smell. That only could come from one place—the foul drool of Elephant Man."

The two looked at the glass and then around the area to see which way to go. They both see that the fused glass went down the fallen tree along the path. So without saying a word, they continued down the path.

The path was overgrown on the edges. It was only wide enough for one creature to walk through at a time. Hugo and Mush pushed on forward slowly, one behind the other. As they came around a bend, they saw a watchman or, in this case, a watch creature. They crouched near a huge oak tree.

Hugo looked at the watchman. "It's Coily. He must be on the lookout for whomever comes by. Mush, can you get passed him and see what has been going on?"

Mush got low to the ground and mushed himself into an oak leaf. "Now blow as hard as you can, and I will pass Coily in this leaf and then continue to the lair. Wait here for me. I will be back soon." Hugo took a deep breath in then got down on the ground and blew the leaf toward Coily.

Coily was a short creature. He looked like a bunch of coils put together with a head on it. He had no hair, but his arms and legs were like a normal human size compared to his body.

The leaf floated past Coily, who looked down at it as if it were an intruder. Coily attempted to step on the leaf but missed and then ignored the leaf. The leaf came to a stop a few feet past Coily, who was looking the other way as a guard should be.

Mush "unmushed" out of the leaf but stayed under the leaf to see where he was and what else was around him. In front of Mush was a steel gate. Within the gate was where his Fallen Brothers resided. Mush got out from under the leaf and mushed through the metal bars in the gate. He hid near a rock and looked around to see where to go next.

Mush saw this fabulous castle on top of a pyramid. Around the pyramid was some sort of moat filled with some type of white liquid. In front of the moat was grass and then a path of rocks, which Mush was hiding in, and then the steel fence and gate. Mush looked in the path of rocks and found two small pebbles, which he mushed into himself. He then crept through the path of rocks and into the grass.

He made his way to the moat of white liquid. Mush dropped one of the pebbles into the white liquid. The pebble floated for a second and then sunk. It also created a ripple in the white liquid, creating bubbles like hot boiling lava. Mush needed to find a way to get to the other side of the moat.

Mush went back to the gate and mushed back through. Mush looked to see what Coily was doing. When Coily looked the other way, Mush picked up the leaf and mushed back through the gate again. Mush got to the moat; he then mushed himself flat to the shape of the leaf, hoping that the leaf will float, and he will have time to get across the moat before it sinks. Mush laid on the leaf. With the last pebble, Mush threw the pebble into the moat to make a ripple. He then sent himself on the leaf and into the moat. The ripple of the pebble and the boiling white stuff sent the leaf across the moat to the other side. Mush unflatten himself and jumped onto the pyramid just as the leaf began to sink into the white liquid.

The steps of the pyramid were too large for Mush to climb up, so Mush mushed himself into a long inchworm-type creature and inched his way to the top of the pyramid one step at a time. The top the pyramid was flat, and so Mush "unmushed" himself as the inchworm creature and back into himself.

Thus far, Mush had not encountered any of his Fallen Brothers other than Coily the watchman. Mush surveyed the area. There was one way into the castle—through the front door. The front door was comprised of two large doors, rounded at the top. They met in the middle and seemed to open inward. Each door was wooden with wrought-iron circular decorations all down the doors. The two handles were large, thick wrought-iron rings. Near the tops of the doors were little windows. The windows had gates on them and were wood so that you cannot see through them unless opened from inside.

Mush decided to climb up the wrought-iron decorations to get to the wooden window. Once at the window, Mush went through the wrought-iron bars and then squeezed through the tiniest crack in the window. He then slithered down the inside of the door and stood flat against the door. Mush surveyed the castle. Inside the castle foyer were all kinds of gold statues and marble pillars. It looked like Mush's Fallen Brothers had been squandering the world up top for centuries.

Mush saw that there were three hallways off the main foyer. Mush followed the hallway to the right. It led down a small corridor and then wound down to a basement. Mush stopped at the last step and peered around the corner. He saw another guard. It was Fish Face. He was tall like Hugo and had two legs. One of his legs ended with a foot but no toes. The other leg ended with a foot that had four toes and was webbed. He could use this foot as a hand. He had no arms. He had a long face with a huge nose. Billows came out on both sides of his face, which went in and out as he breathes.

Fish Face was guarding six rooms—three on the right side and three on the left side. The basement was made of a dirt floor with little pebbles. So Mush mushed himself into a pebble and slowly rolled past Fish Face to the first room on the right. Fish Face did not move.

Mush peered into the first room. He saw a few small children laying on hay. On the other side of the hall, Mush saw several kinds of animals, each in their own cage. Mush continued to the second room on the right. Once again, he found several children in the room on the right and across the hall were several kinds of animals, each in their own cages. Mush made it down to the last rooms and found all kinds of toys and candy in the room on the right. On the other side were all kinds of animal treats and toys. At the end of the corridor was another guard, who looked exactly like Fish Face. *It must be his twin*, thought Mush. Then there was another staircase winding up. Mush got to the bottom of the staircase, and once the guard was looking the other way, Mush "unmushed" himself and made his way, winding up, to the top of the staircase.

Only running into two of his Fallen Brothers, Mush decided to leave the castle with the information that he had before he ran into any more of his Fallen Brothers. Mush got to the front door and could get out the same way he got in. The inside of the door looked exactly like the outside.

Once at the bottom of the pyramid, Mush needed to figure out how to get back across the moat. With no leaves around, Mush morphed into a fly and flew across the moat. Once across the moat, Mush morphed back into his own body.

Mush made it to the steel gate and mushed himself through. He waited to see what Coily was doing. Mush slowly made his way toward Coily, mushing himself into the ground after every step so as not to be spotted by Coily. As Mush was right under Coily, Coily looked down at the ground but only saw ground. Mush stayed still.

Hugo was watching and waiting the entire time. Seeing that Mush may have a small problem, Hugo blew another leaf past Coily. Coily once again looked at the leaf as if it were an intruder. At the same time, Mush made his way to Hugo. The two of them made their way back to Lilim.

Chapter 9

Meanwhile, Rooty and Snailstein made their way to the start of the root system. They went through the big lighted area and down the tunnel of light and to the cave entrance. They then proceeded to morph themselves into the root system and made their way to the top world.

Rooty looked at Snailstein. "I am going back to into the root system, and I will go through the other roots to see what I can find. You can find something small and alive and take it through the root system with you."

Snailstein replied in his deep, distinguished voice, "I will go through and morph with an animal the first time. The second time, I will morph but let the animal go through on its own accord. We will meet back here. How long do you need to go through the root system?"

Rooty was puzzled. "I'm not sure. You just wait here until I get back." Rooty then disappears into the roots.

Snailstein began to look for a small animal to help with his experiment. Snailstein did not have to look far. He found an ant just as he took his first step. Snailstein, with his long tentacle arms, picked up the ant. Snailstein talked to the ant. "I will be kind and only take you for a little while to do my experiment."

Snailstein then morphed with the ant and went through the root system to the tunnel's entrance. The ant came out the same as it was in the top world. Quickly, Snailstein went back up top to do it again. This time Snailstein morphed himself and grabbed the ant without morphing it and both of them went into the root system. Once again, the ant came out exactly how it was in the top world. Once again, he quickly went back to the top world. This did not explain how the children came out smaller when they morphed or how they would return to the top world.

Snailstein began to think of how he could demonstrate what happened to the children. Once up on the top world, Snailstein began to look around for something a little bigger, but not too big, to go through the root system. Snailstein found a baby mouse only a few feet into the woods. The baby mouse was a little bigger than Snailstein.

The mouse seemed curious and followed Snailstein, wanting to play. Snailstein morphed with the mouse and made their way down to the cave. Once in the cave and seeing that the mouse was the same size that it had been, Snailstein morphed with the mouse back to the top world. Snailstein then did not morph himself but did morph the mouse. When they arrived back in the cave, the mouse was smaller. The mouse was the size a normal mouse would be if Lilim had mice, which they do not.

Snailstein now had the proof that he needed in how the children got to Lilim and how they were the size they were. Snailstein tried to get the mouse back up to the top world. He morphed and tried to pull the mouse back up, but it would not go through the root system. Stumped on how to get the mouse back to the top world, Snailstein brought the mouse to One Arm who is always waiting to greet anyone that comes his way. "Watch over this mouse here in the white lighted area. I will be back soon with Rooty, and we will go see Tall One," exclaimed Snailstein with his deep, distinguished voice. "Welcome to Lilim," replied One Arm.

Snailstein waited in the top world near the entrance to the root system. All the while, Rooty was making his way through the root system with exceptional speed. Rooty would stop at different exits along the root system to see what was going on in that part of the world. The root system was like a superhighway for Lilith's children. Rooty had not seen any differences in any of the roots that he had been through compared to the ones near Lilim. After covering all the roots he possibly could, Rooty returned to the top world where Snailstein was waiting. As Rooty popped up, he heard in that deep, distinguished voice. "Find anything?"

Rooty replied, "No. How about you?"

Snailstein morphed and went down the root system to the cave with Rooty following. "Welcome to Lilim!" said One Arm with a tiny mouse next to him. Snailstein, with his deep, distinguished voice, exclaimed, "It's us One Arm. I will take the mouse with me, and we will go see Tall One."

Chapter 10

mil and Shelly were being entertained by Big Floppy Ears, showing them around and introducing them to all the creatures of Lilim. They had been all through the village and were on their way to Hugo's Grill and Café when they saw Hugo, Rooty, Mush, and Snailstein enter the village.

Once they were all at Hugo's Grill and Café, Tall One appeared. "What have you found on the root system and our Fallen Brothers? And what is that thing in your tentacle, Snailstein?"

Snailstein replied in his deep, distinguishing voice, "If one morphs with a being live or inanimate, the item will morph with you and come out on our side, the same as if it were on the top world. If, however, you do not morph, but morph the object that is alive, it will come out as it was on the top world but will be in a size in relevance to our size. And then you cannot take it back to the top world, hence the mouse." Silence fell upon all those at Hugo's Grill and Café.

Tall One looked around the café. "This is most interesting. Rooty, what did you find in the root system itself?"

Rooty began, "I traveled through all the root system that I possibly could. I also stopped at numerous exits and went to the top world to see if anything there was disturbed. I found nothing. All of the top world and the root system are intact and as I have built them."

Silence again fell over those at Hugo's Grill and Café. Once again, Tall One surveyed the crowd and began, "This does not tell us a whole lot except that ourselves and our Fallen Brothers can travel through the root system without any concerns. We can also bring inanimate and live things through the root system whenever we want. Hugo, I hope that you and Mush have come up with something."

Hugo began, "We found a place where some of our Fallen Brothers reside close to us—in our forest. In the middle of the steep cliff, you only have to travel a short distance from the root system's entrance to find their watchman."

Mush then continued, "After the watchman is a large steel fence and gate. Wrought-iron fence and gate that is as big as if you were on the top world. However, the rails are close enough together that one cannot slip through them, except if you morph or in my case mush. If you make it through that, there is a path of rocks around their fortress. Over the rocks, you come to a path of grass that surrounds the moat. The moat is filled with a white liquid that bubbles like boiling hot lava if something is dropped in it. On the other side of the moat is a pyramid of steps and on top of the steps is a castle in which our Fallen Brothers reside. The castle is filled with gold statues and marble columns. There are three hallways off the main foyer. I only had time to follow one hallway. This one led to a basement with six cages—three on either side of the corridor. In them I found children, small like Emil and Shelly. I mean, small in relation to their size on the top world. I also found several kinds of animals. There were two cages of each of these. The last two cages were filled with candy, toys, and treats to lure the children and animals. I got out fast and did not see any of our Fallen Brothers except the two guards in the basement, Fish Face and his twin. Oh, and Coily, who was guarding the path to the castle."

Everyone in Hugo's Grill and Café began whispering to each other. Emil and Shelly were shocked. They looked at each other not knowing how to react. Shelly took hold of Emil's hand.

Tall One again surveyed the crowd and then began, "I do not know how Emil and Shelly will get home. We will put our best creatures on it and continue to work on the way to get them home. However, our Fallen Brothers have been pillaging the top world for quite some time. Taking anything that they please, including children. Now they know that we know since we have Emil and Shelly. We must fortify our cave and prepare for battle. Our Fallen Brothers will soon be coming for our guests."

Chapter 11

s every creature took off to do their best to fortify the cave, Shelly and Emil were left at Hugo's Grill and Café with One Arm. "What do we do now?" questioned Shelly, still holding onto Emil's hand.

"I don't know," replied Emil.

"You help us to fortify the cave," stated One Arm.

"Yes, of course, we will help to fortify the cave. What would you like us to do?" asked Shelly as she let go of Emil's hand. One Arm led then to the river. He left Shelly with the children of Lilim to help them. Shelly was helping the children to put porcupine quills, like spikes, on the river's edge to keep out intruders. There were hills surrounding one side of the river and a braided rope-like edge on the other side. This is where they were putting the quills.

One Arm then took Emil to the front of the cave. "Here," said One Arm.

"Here what?" asked Emil.

"Here, you need to start here and figure out how to close the entrance to make it look like it's not a cave and there is no way in," responded One Arm.

"How do I do that?" asked Emil, but One Arm had already left. Emil was trying to come up with a way to camouflage the entrance to the cave but could not come up with anything. As he paced back and forth in front of the cave near the mushroom patch and one of the children of Lilim came up behind Emil and began to pace with him.

"What are you doing?" asked this little creature. This little creature looked like some sort of bird.

Emil was startled. "I…I…I am trying to think of a way to camouflage the entrance to the cave."

The bird like creature then asked, "So this is how humans come up with ideas? They just don't pop into your head like ours do?"

Emil, getting annoyed, now spoke a little sterner. "I am pacing because it helps me to think. And who are you anyway? And why are you here and not with the other children?"

"I am Birdy, and I don't want to be a child. So I thought you could use some help," said Birdy.

Emil continued to pace, and Birdy did so too. "Maybe we can use these mushrooms to cover the entrance to the cave so that it looks like one big mushroom patch with no entrance," exclaimed Emil.

"Okay," said Birdy. "And how do we do that?"

"I am not sure yet," replied Emil. Just then, One Arm appeared, "That's a good idea. We can get some mushrooms from above and place them here within the mushroom patch and close up the entrance to the cave. Then we need to come up with a way to fortify the inside of the cave in case our Fallen Brothers find the entrance through the mushroom patch. You two continue to come up with more ideas, and I will get the others to fortify the mushroom patch with more mushrooms to camouflage the cave entrance." With a turn, One Arm was gone.

Emil and Birdy began to pace again, back and forth, in front of the cave entrance. Emil was thinking out loud. "When we came down the cliff, it seemed to be a steep cliff, but it was indeed a slight incline. And we did not see the mushroom patch until we had gotten past the waving ferns. Then we only saw the entrance to the cave once we got through the mushroom patch."

Birdy replied, "So what does that have to do with anything?"

"I wasn't talking to you…I was thinking," replied Emil.

"Well, you said it out loud, and I still do not understand what you are talking about," spouted Birdy.

Emil began, "I was thinking if you don't see the cave until you get through the mushroom patch, and we are making the mushroom patch denser so that you wouldn't know there was a cave, then all we need to do is make the edge of the mushroom patch by the entrance to the cave hidden."

"I know that, so what are you talking about?" responded confused Birdy.

Emil began to laugh. "Ha, ha, ha, I have an idea, but I don't know how to build it because it makes no sense."

Just as before, One Arm appeared without a warning. "What is this idea that makes no sense?"

Emil, unsure how to answer, said, "How do you keep popping up when I talk about an idea?"

One Arm replied, "I just know, so what is your idea?"

Emil began, "When we got to the bottom of the root system, as you call it. We, Shelly and I, ended up in a white lighted area. There was no wall behind us that we could see, but we could not go in that direction. So if we can use that technology, or whatever you call it, we could camouflage the entrance to the cave behind the mushroom patch."

One Arm stood quietly for a moment. "I will go talk to Rooty. You two stay here and help the others that come with the mushrooms. Help make it as dense of a mushroom patch as you can."

The creatures of Lilim returned with the mushrooms. Emil, Birdy, and the rest of the creatures began to fill in the mushroom patch. This took most of the day; it was getting late, and everyone was tired. When they finished up, the creatures told Emil and Birdy to go back to Hugo's Grill and Café. Everyone was gathering there for further instructions from Tall One.

Shelly was helping the children finish with the last of the porcupine quills on the inner side of the river when Emil showed up with Birdy. "Who is your friend?" questioned Shelly.

Emil replied, "Birdy, one of the children that was supposed to be helping you, followed me. We are heading to Hugo's Grill and Café. Everyone is supposed to meet there for further instructions from Tall One." Without saying a word, Shelly motioned to the children, and they all followed Emil and Birdy to Hugo's Grill and Café.

All the creatures were lining up and getting plates of food from Hugo as he was grilling. Emil and Shelly got in line and, after getting a plate of food, found a place to sit down away from the others. Shelly turned to Emil, who was stuffing his face with food. "How are we ever going to get home? This place is nice and all, but it's not home. Our parents are probably going out of their minds. It has been over a day, and we are gone. What are we going to do?"

Emil stopped chewing for a moment and then swallowed. "There is nothing we can do. This is a real adventure. Not one that I made up in my head. I know that our parents are probably worried, but we can't do anything about it. And once Tall One has told us what everyone is to do next, I will speak to him about getting home. Now eat something."

"Okay," replied Shelly as she took a bite of food, wondering what exactly she was eating but was too worried about home to ask what it was.

As everyone was finishing their food, Tall One appeared. "You have all been very busy trying to fortify and save our Lilim." Without a warning, there was a deep groan and then a rumble under everyone's feet. Thinking that it was the start of an attack by our Fallen Brothers, everyone in the village ran to their positions of defense. The littlest ones hid in their houses. However, the biggest children lined up by the river with porcupine quills in hand as spears.

The rumble stopped! No one had tried to enter the cave. Tall One signaled to Hugo, Rooty, Mush, and Snailstein. They all immediately returned to the café. "Go out through the dense mushroom patch and past the ferns and see what is going on," urged Tall One. The four of them took off immediately without a word. At first, nothing seemed different. As they headed farther up the path, Rooty and Snailstein took to the root system, while Hugo and Mush headed toward the residence of their Fallen Brothers.

As Hugo and Mush rounded the corner where they had seen the guard Coily, they come upon and awful sight. The moat around the pyramid was burning. Huge flames were spurting up into the air. It looked as if the entire pyramid was engulfed in flames, yet it was not; it was surrounded by flames shooting up through the milky white liquid. Coily and several other guards were staring at the fire from outside the gate. You could see no life on the other side atop the pyramid around the castle.

Hugo motioned to Mush. "We have to go and get some help to see what started this." The two of them made their way back to the cave. Rooty and Snailstein flashed through the root system and peeked up top but found nothing different. They also made their way back to the cave. Once again, they gathered at the café. Hugo and Mush explained what they had seen. "I have to get a closer look to see what ignited the liquid like that," exclaimed Mush. Tall One ordered everyone back to their posts in case of an attack. He then told Hugo to take Mush and the Mush brothers back to the pyramid.

Chapter 12

Mush and his brothers, Musher and Mushy, went with Hugo and returned to the gate. The guards were still preoccupied with the flames. Mush and the Mush brothers mushed through the gate. They slowly crept through the rocks toward the grass. They moved to the left of the castle's door. The guards seemed to be fixated on that area of the castle. The ground was getting warmer and warmer as Mush and his Mush brothers pushed toward the moat. When they got as close as they could to the moat, they could see that the liquid was not burning. Yet the fire was burning just above the white lava like liquid. The Mush brothers carefully took samples of the white liquid, the earth near the moat, and the earth in the moat. They slowly mushed themselves with little vials in hand and collected the samples. As they were finishing, they could see the guards walking around the back of the castle. Mush and his brothers took their vials and headed back to the gate. Together with Hugo, they went back to Lilim to study the vials of liquid and dirt. As Mush and his Mush brothers went back to the lab to see Snailstein, Hugo went and told Tall One what they had found at the castle and that it was not an attack on Lilim yet.

At the lab, they started to look at the samples. "The liquid sample is cold. The last time I encountered this white liquid, it bubbled and burned the leaf that I had floated on. What could turn a lava-like liquid cold, yet there were flames atop of it," questioned Mush.

Snailstein, in his deep, distinguished voice, said, "I have a thought. Dry ice is cold, yet the vapors are carbon dioxide. Maybe they added something to cause the vapors to burn."

"Why would they want to place a fire ring around the castle? Who are they trying to keep out?" questioned Mush.

"We need to let Tall One know of our findings and see what he thinks. What about the earth, Snailstein?" continued Mush.

Snailstein replied, "It is as I thought. It seems as if some sort of dry ice was used to make the steam. I am still not sure about the flames, the heat, or the fire atop the moat. Maybe it is dry ice with a flammable compound added. I'm not sure, but it's irrelevant. We still need to find out what our Fallen Brothers are up to. Go see Tall One, and I will continue to see what else I can find out."

Mush and the Mush brothers went back to the café and told Tall One about the liquid and the questions they still had. Tall One answered, "Our Fallen Brothers know that we have Emil and Shelly. They probably know that we know where their castle is. This is probably to protect themselves."

Emil and Shelly had been listening to all the possibilities from the creatures of Lilim. "Why haven't they attacked us if they know we are here?" questioned Emil.

"They don't know that we are here," exclaimed Shelly.

Tall One responded, "You are wise, Shelly. We need to go back and see what our Fallen Brothers are really up to. Hugo, take Mush and the Mush brothers and go around the moat and see what we are missing."

Once again, Hugo, Mush, and the Mush brothers head to the pyramid. The guards were gone, but the flames were still burning. Hugo stayed at the gate again while Mush and the Mush brothers proceeded toward the moat. Once at the moat, they followed it around to the left. The entire moat was engulfed surrounding the pyramid.

"Oh," whispered Mush to his brothers. "Look at the back side of the pyramid. There is another way out. A drawbridge of sorts. We have to cross and see what is going on in the castle." Musher agreed to go along with Mush, and Mushy went back to Hugo to let him know what Mush was up to. Hugo demanded that they stay and wait for Mush and Musher. Mushy debated and decided to go back to the cave and let Tall One know what they had found. Hugo stayed to wait for Mush and Musher.

As Mush and Musher got closer to the drawbridge, they could see that the flames had stopped near the drawbridge on both sides. It made a great escape route out of the castle. Mush and Musher went over the drawbridge and into the castle where they saw only one main hall down the center of the castle. There were works of art all along the walls on both sides. The two brothers slowly got to the end of the hall, which brought them back to the main foyer of the castle. Mush told his brother, "Go to the hallway on the right. That will take you downstairs to where the children and pets are kept. I will go explore the hallway to the left and meet you back here."

Musher slowly went down the hallway steps. At the last step, he peered around the corner expecting to see Fish Face, but there was no one there. Musher went past the first room. "Empty," he says to himself. He continued to the next room, and again, there was nothing but hay scattered across the floor. He continued to the last room and again found nothing. No treats or toys or guards. Musher wound his way up the staircase and down the hall to the foyer.

Meanwhile, Mush took the hallway to the left. This hallway went upstairs instead of down. Mush slowly went up the steps and stopped at the top step to peer around the corner—no guard. This hallway was like the other hallway with three rooms on either side of the hall, but these had doors not cages. Mush slowly moved to the first room. There were four beds in both rooms on either side of the hall. He then moved to the next two rooms. One room was a kitchen-type setup and the other was a dining area. Mush then went to the last two rooms at the end of the hallway. Both doors were closed. Mush decided to go into the room on the right first. He mushed under the door and looked around and saw books and maps of the upper world. There were papers scattered all over the place as if someone was in a hurry and they took what they could carry and left. Mush went back out and mushed under the door across the hall. This room had one bed in it and looked scattered like the other room. Mush went down the steps and back to the foyer where Musher was waiting.

The two Mush brothers went back down the hall of the castle and back over the drawbridge. The moat was still burning, and the flames did not seem to be dying down. As they walked over the draw-bridge, they saw a path through the woods. Mush and Musher went to start down the path, and once again, there was fused glass along the path. "Elephant Man was here and look at those tracks. Looks like some sort of cart," responded Mush when his brother looked at him.

"What did you find?"

"Nothing," replied Musher.

"Same here," said Mush.

"And it seems as if they have taken everything down that path, but to where?" Mush motioned to his brother, and they both began to walk back and found Hugo waiting for them. "We must go back to Lilim and speak to Tall One," stated Mush. And with that, the three of them made their way back to Lilim.

Chapter 13

At the café, Mush explained, "Everything was gone. No guards, no children, no animals, no toys, or treats. Everything gone. I also went up the other hallway, which went upstairs. There were three rooms on either side of the hallway, but they had doors. There were two bedrooms, enough to sleep eight. So two guards for the upper hallway and two guards for the lower hallway. Then Coily, Elephant Man, and room for two more guards, the ones at the gate with Coily. Then there was a kitchen and dining area, a stately bedroom for the leader. And then a study across the hall with books and maps. It looked as if they knew we were around and left in a hurry. Behind the drawbridge was an escape route. The big castle had just twelve rooms and a hallway with all kinds of art still on the walls.

Tall One responded, "Our Fallen Brothers have left, but we still must be on guard. They do not know where we are, but they know we are close. We will send a group to see where the path leads in the morning, but for now let's study what we have." Snailstein, Rooty, Mush, and Hugo left the café and went to the lab. Emil followed.

Shelly stayed with Tall One and asked, "I know that there is a lot going on here in Lilim. But are we ever going to get back home?"

Tall One looked at Shelly and patted her on the head. "We will sift through all the evidence and come up with a plan to help you and see what our Fallen Brothers are up to. For now, relax and let the others do the worrying."

Once in the lab, Emil walked around and poked at everything he could get his hand on. "Leave that stuff alone!" exclaimed Snailstein with his deep, distinguished voice.

"Sorry," replied Emil as he put down the glass jar filled with blue liquid. The four of them sat down and began discussing what they had learned. Meanwhile, Emil was still wandering around the lab and still touching everything.

Rooty began, "First, we know that our Fallen Brothers have discovered that they can get through the root system like us. Second, they can take items from the upper world and bring them below."

Snailstein interjected, "They have been pillaging for years!"

"Right," replied Rooty. "Third, they can pull humans and animals down the root system and make them our size. But we cannot bring them back up."

Emil was looking at the mouse that they had brought back and questioned, "What happened when you tried to bring the mouse back up to my world?"

Snailstein started, "Without morphing the mouse, it came down and it was smaller. The normal size a mouse would be if we had mice in Lilim. When I tried to pull this mouse up top, it would not go. I could not move it."

Emil questioned again, "Did you try morphing the mouse and yourself together to go to my world?"

Snailstein replied, "No, that would make the mouse the size it is now but in the top world. It would be the size of a bug."

Emil now with a smirk on his face again questioned, "But did you try it?"

Snailstein looked perplexed and, again, replied, "No, what would that do?"

Emil began, "I know that I am just a kid but think outside the box. What if that would reverse it, and you could pull the mouse up top? Maybe it would even go back to its original size."

They all looked at each other. Hugo, still a little confused, said, "I will go talk to Tall One, but we still need to get a group together to see where our Fallen Brothers have gone and what is our next step in dealing with them. Do we just leave the children like Emil and Shelly with them to do whatever?" With that, Hugo left and went to see Tall One.

Hugo met up with Tall One at the café and explained what Emil had proposed. Tall One responded, "Get a group together to search for our Fallen Brothers and leave Rooty and Snailstein to try Emil's plan. You leave at first light."

Emil had come up behind Hugo and shouted, "I will go to see where your Fallen Brothers have gone."

Hugo jumped when Emil shouted and turned to look at Tall One. Tall One stated, "That's kind of you, but we do not know what we will be up against or how far they have gone."

"The more reason for me to go," replied Emil.

"I can help the children if you find them, and if they have other children, I should be able to go the route they took. And Shelly can help with the mouse. We don't even know if it will work, but maybe they can find us a way home. Until then, I want to help."

"It is settled then," stated Tall One. "Get some rest. You all leave at first light. Hugo, tell the others the plan. Bring Mush and the Mush brothers with you tomorrow."

Hugo left to tell the others the plan. Meanwhile, Emil found Shelly and told her the plan. As they settled in for the night, Shelly asked, "Do you think we can really find a way home?"

"Sure, we got here so there needs to be a way back," replied Emil. "You will go with Snailstein and Rooty to find a way home. I am going to help the other children if we can find them. So maybe they can go home too."

Shelly, now yawning, said, "You be careful. We don't know what's out there."

Emil, returning the yawn, replied, "I will. You just find a way home." At that, they both fell asleep.

Chapter 14

Emil was up before light. He slowly crept out of the basket shelter and made his way to find Hugo and the Mush brothers. There was a quiet peace about Lilim. Emil strolled down by the stream. *This was nothing like home,* Emil thought.

Just then, Birdy replied, "Tell me what your home is like."

Startled and puzzled, Emil questioned, "Where did you come from? Did I say that out loud?"

Birdy replied, "I followed you and yes."

Emil, still puzzled that he had actually said that out loud, said, "Why are you here? I have an important mission to go on."

Birdy responded, "When I heard about the mission, I spoke to Hugo. He told me that since I helped you with the mushroom patch, I could help with this. So what is so different about your world?"

Emil began, "You have never been to my world?"

"No," stated Birdy.

"Oh," said Emil and then he began again. "We do not have Fallen Brothers. We do not have anyone chasing us. All the things down here that you use are ten times bigger in my world. The house basket that we stay in here is like my mom's laundry basket. We each have our own mom and our own family. Our streams have woods around them. Shelly and I pretend that we are knights looking for dragons to slay. We run around with our pretend swords and…and…and…this happens. Our adventure has become real, and Shelly is afraid that we will never see our parents again."

Hugo appeared with the Mush brothers. "Are you ready?"

"Yes," replied Birdy.

"I have to let Shelly know that I am leaving." stated Emil.

"Go then, and we will meet up with you at the mushroom patch. Emil ran back to the basket to wake Shelly and let her know that he was leaving. Shelly was already awake and on her way out of the basket to go find Snailstein and Rooty.

"I'm leaving," said Emil when he saw Shelly.

Shelly turned and said, "I'm on my way to find Snailstein and Rooty. Wish me luck, and I will see you when you get back. Be careful." Shelly and Emil began walking away from each other. Shelly looked back at Emil, but he continued forth. As Shelly turned back and headed to Hugo's Grill and Café, Emil turned to see Shelly walking into the café.

Chapter 15

Emil met up with Birdy, Hugo, and the Mush brothers at the mushroom patch. They made their way through the mushrooms, past the ferns, and up the path toward the castle. As they went past the fallen branch and got closer to the castle, they could see no guard and no flames. Just an eerie mist of smoke and fog. They all paused at the gate. The mush brothers were the only ones who could mush through the gate. Birdy flew over. Hugo grabbed Emil in a bear hug, and before Emil could blink, they morphed through the gate. "That was cool," replied Emil as he patted himself to see if he was all there. Over the rocks and across the grass, and then around to the moat to the left, they made their way to the drawbridge and still no one in sight.

As they made their way into the woods from across the drawbridge, they saw a way out of the gate. The gate on this side was wide open, inviting Hugo and his team to go forward and deeper into the woods. The path was wide enough to pull a cart through. Each side of the path was overgrown with thick briar bushes. The bushes had thorns all over them and red berries. The bushes were dense and so close together, you could not get through them. It looked like they were planted tight together in order to create this path. Beyond the bushes, you could see trees behind and above them.

Hugo began talking to no one in particular, "They must have pulled a cart through this. See the tire ruts. The castle must have just been a stopover until they had a place for the children." Everyone was listening, but no one responded. They followed the path and shards of glass that Elephant Man's drool had fused and left behind. They had walked for an hour seeing nothing but the path that they were on and the woods of thistle. So dense. So thick. Hugo bean again, "I hope that this is not an ambush. The only way out is back. There is nowhere to hide, and now we have been walking for about two hours. And we have seen nothing."

Mush interjected, "Me and Musher will forge ahead while you take a rest. We can mush into anything and see what's ahead without being detected."

"Good," replied Hugo. "We will rest for ten minutes and then follow. This way, we can be of help to you if needed or retreat if needed."

Mush and Musher continued forward, walking past the dense thistle. After about three hours, they came to a field of grass. It opened so wide, all you could see was grass and the path that the rolling cart made. Mush and Musher decided to wait for the others before continuing. The others arrived ten minutes later.

"Wow, grass as far as the eye can see," responded Birdy.

Mush responded, "We waited before going any further without you."

Hugo replied, "Good. Let us continue forth and see where this leads."

After walking for another half hour, the tracks disappeared, vanished as if they were never there. Hugo stopped suddenly and scratched his head, "Birdy, fly a little father and see if you can pick up the trail."

Birdy took off without responding and flew for a while making a big circle outward. All Birdy could see was grass as far as the eye could see. Birdy flew back down and landed next to Emil, "There was only grass as far as the eye could see. No path. It just ends here."

Mush and his brothers all looked at each other and then at Hugo. Hugo responds, "We have nowhere to go from here right now. It's at least a three-and-a-half-hour trip back to the castle. Let us go back to the castle and see what we can find on their maps. Maybe they will tell us where the path went." They all turned around and headed back to the castle.

They returned to the castle tired. All of them went to the map room with Mush leading the way. Once in the map room, they all began looking at what was left of the books and maps. Most of the maps were of the upper world. They each took a section of the room and began looking methodically at all of the maps and books.

"I found something!" yelled Emil.

"Let me see," replied Hugo.

"It's a map, but it looks as if it is of the root system. Oh, this is not good. Rooty will not like this. He will not like this at all."

Mush then said, "Let's see what else we can find because we still have not found where the path leads. We will spend another hour and then go back to the cave with what we have."

Everyone agreed and began, once again, looking at the books and maps. After the hour was up, Hugo stated "It's time to leave. We need to go and let Tall One know what we have and have not found."

As Birdy took flight to leave the room, he said, "Wait, look at this little scrap." Birdy flew down and picked up the scrap in his claws. "It looks like a trail. I can't tell what trail because it's only a small part. But if it's a piece from the path we were on, maybe it will be of some use."

"Good eye." replied Hugo. "Let's take everything that we have back to Tall One."

Chapter 16

Shelly met up with Snailstein and Rooty at the café. "Where is the baby mouse?" asked Shelly.

"We have to pick it up on the way," replied Snailstein in his deep, distinguished voice. They all went to the lab and picked up the mouse. As they made their way down the path to the root system, Shelly began to worry about Elephant Man or someone like him showing up.

Snailstein, sensing her apprehension, assured Shelly, "Nothing will happen here, and we will all be fine. Rooty made up this root system, and it was unexpected that you dropped in, but nothing will harm you." Shelly smiled but was still weary. Once they got to the beginning of the root system, Rooty stated, "I will go up top alone and make sure all is safe before we begin our experiment.

Rooty went up the root system and noticed something odd. At the exact spot that Shelly and Emil had come down, on the root was a mark. Some sort of scar within the root. It was a tiny mark, but a mark nonetheless. Rooty went back and told Snailstein about the mark. Snailstein replied, "Go look at the other roots and see if you can find the same marks. Maybe this will tell us where the other children came from before we start our experiment."

Rooty went like a flash and throughout the root system found similar marks all over the root system. Little scars all over the world. Rooty made his way back to Snailstein and reported what he had found. Snailstein replied, "I will tell Tall One and you begin the experiment."

Rooty took the mouse and morphed the mouse with himself. Both of them were on the top world, but the mouse was like Snailstein had thought—it was tiny. The size it was in Lilim. Rooty couldn't leave it there that size and returned with the mouse.

Shelly, a little excited, asked, "Did it work?"

"No, I'm sorry, Shelly. We will find another way to get you and Emil home. Let us go see Tall One," replied Rooty. They both walked quietly with the mouse back to see Tall One.

Tall One was sitting with Snailstein when Shelly and Rooty arrived at the café. "No luck with the mouse and our experiment," stated Rooty.

"Are the scars permanent in the root or will they heal?" asked Tall One.

"I believe that they are permanent because in some of the roots the scars are deeper. And in others, there is more than one scar. I do not know how I missed this when I went through the root system the last time. This also creates a dilemma because it may eventually destroy the roots themselves, and therefore, our root system of travel," responded Rooty.

Tall One sat quietly for a moment. He then began, "We need to sit down with Hugo and Mush to see what they have found out about our Fallen Brothers. This will affect all of us. We will meet tonight after dinner, back here, to discuss our options."

Mush, Musher, Mushy, Hugo, Emil, and Birdy all made it back to the café and told Tall One what they had seen. Tall One told them what Rooty, Shelly, and Snailstein had found out. Tall One then told them to have some dinner and meet up afterward to discuss what could be done.

Chapter 17

Shelly and Emil met by the river to eat their dinner. Shelly began, "Your idea did not work. The mouse was too tiny when they got up to the top world, our world."

Emil looked at Shelly and put his head on hers. "We will find a way to get back home. We lost the trail of the Fallen Brothers in a field. It was like they had vanished into thin air."

Shelly put her head in her hands. "What are we going to do? I don't know if we will ever get home. Do you think our parents are worried?"

Emil shook his head. "I try not to think about our parents and what is going on at home. We will find a way back, but for now, we need to think about how to help our new friends of Lilim."

Shelly looked up at Emil. "I agree. Let's go to the café and see if we can help come up with some ideas." Emil stood up and offered his hand to Shelly. Shelly took his hand, and Emil pulled her up to her feet. They walked side by side back to the café.

When they arrived at the café, Tall One was already there with Rooty and Snailstein. They all sat quietly until Hugo, Mush, Birdy, and the Mush brothers arrived. Tall One began, "We have three dilemmas that we need to address before we continue with any plans. First, our root system has scars and may be compromised as a way of travel if our Fallen Brothers continue to bring children and animals down the root system. Second, our Fallen Brothers have vanished. So how do we proceed with our Fallen Brothers? And third, we still have not found a way to get our friends, Shelly and Emil, back to their home. All these are important to us. Where do we start and what can we do about these problems?"

Mush spoke up, "It took us four hours to get to the field where our Fallen Brothers disappeared."

Rooty chimed in, "It looks as if every time our Fallen Brothers have brought back a child to our world from the top world, it has created a scar in the root. Eventually, it will destroy the root system and therefore destroy whatever the root is attached to in the top world."

Emil stood up. "Us—Shelly and I—being here has brought a light on a lot of things for the inhabitants of Lilim. The only way to find a way home for us is to find out and somehow stop your Fallen Brothers from destroying the root system. I believe that if we find a way to deal with your Fallen Brothers, then we will also find a way home. So Shelly and myself are up to helping out."

Everyone looked at each other, but no one spoke. Then Tall One stood up. "Very well. Mush will get a team together, and you will venture out and find out what happened to the trail and our Fallen Brothers. Bring enough supplies to last you a week. If you do not find them within three days, return to Lilim. Snailstein and Rooty, you two go over everything that we have about the root system. Try to find a way to stop the scars or help heal them and a way home for Shelly and Emil."

Chapter 18

Early the next morning, Shelly and Emil met up with Mush, Hugo, and Birdy at the café. Mush decided that he and his two brothers would go with Emil, Hugo, and Birdy. He told Shelly to find Snailstein and see if they could come up with an idea to get them home along with any other children they may find. The six of them gathered enough supplies for a week and headed out to the castle of their Fallen Brothers. As they got closer to the castle, they could see no flames, no smoke, and no fog. Just an eerie calm about the castle as if it had been abandoned years ago. Hugo morphed Emil through the gate. The rest went through on their own as Birdy flew over the fence. As they got closer to the drawbridge, they could see that it made for a great escape route out of the castle. They decided to take another look at the maps to see if there was anything about the path behind the castle and where it led to. They went over the drawbridge and into the castle. Finding nothing about the path, the six of them walked out of the castle and headed down the path.

It was close to midday when they reached the field where the trace of their Fallen Brothers had ended. Emil, the Mush brothers, and Hugo looked around and all they could see were miles and miles of yellowish grassy straw-like fields. Mush looked at them all. "We should split up so we can cover more ground and meet back here in two hours. Hugo, you take Emil. Me and my brothers will go the other way. Birdy you can fly between us and maybe pick up something that we cannot see."

Hugo replied, "We will take the right side of the path and you take the left. Do not wander too far from the center."

"I won't" responded Mush. Emil followed Hugo. Although the field of grass was only waist high, Hugo created his own path for Emil to follow. Emil followed but only saw grass all around him. Mush and his brothers took off to the left and saw only grass around them as they went forward. Birdy flew above, but only saw grass as far as the bird's eye view could see.

Birdy flew down to Hugo. "I can only see grass as far as my bird's eye can see."

Emil replied, "Hugo, maybe we should take a closer look at the spot where we lost your Fallen Brothers."

Hugo looked at Birdy and then Emil. "I agree. Let us look where our Fallen Brothers have disappeared. Birdy, go let Mush and his brothers know what we have seen and not seen. And that we are going back to the spot where our Fallen Brothers disappeared. Birdy flew off. Hugo and Emil made their way back. "Do you think that they morphed their way out of here?" questioned Emil. "No." stated Hugo "Even though they could have morphed everyone and everything, I would be able to tell. No. There's another explanation. We just need to take a closer look at where the path stopped."

Birdy flew over to Mush and his brothers, "Hugo and Emil went back to where the path ended. I could see only grass as far as my bird's eye could see. So we decided that there has to be another way they went."

Mush looked at Birdy. "I agree. We have found nothing either. We will meet you back by Hugo and Emil." With that, Birdy flew off, and Mush and his brothers turned around and began making their way back to the beginning of the path.

Emil got down on his hands and knees. He began crawling around, running his hands on the ground where the trail ended, and the golden grass began. Birdy landed on Hugo's shoulder. "That's odd," stated Emil.

"What's odd?" asked Mush as he and his brothers appeared and saw Emil on the ground, on his hands and knees, crawling around.

Emil excitedly said, "There's a bump here. Where the path and grass meet. Maybe it was their way out."

Birdy responded, "Why didn't we think of this before? Maybe we will be able to find where our Fallen Brothers have gone."

"Slow down," replied Mush. "We still need to figure out how to get into wherever it is they have gone."

Emil and Mush began trying to brush the dirt away from the bump. They realized it was some type of door. "It's a door!" exclaimed Emil.

"We need to figure out how this door opens," stated Mush. The Mush brothers joined in, pushing dirt away from the edge. Soon they found more edges. They began to clear off the middle and found a handle and all three edges. Hugo reached down and pulled at the handle to the trapdoor.

"Slowly!' exclaimed Mush "We don't know if it is some kind of trap.

"Okay," replied Hugo as he continued to pull up the door. Everyone else moved back. The trapdoor opened to reveal a ramp leading to a tunnel. "We do not know where this leads or what we may encounter, so I will go first," stated Hugo. "You come last, Emil, and close the door," responded Mush.

They all slowly went down the ramp. "Everyone, turn on your lights. I am going to close the trapdoor now," stated Emil. Everyone turned on their lights as Emil closed the door. Then they slowly trudged down the ramp, which flattened out to a dirt path.

"We are heading back toward the castle," stated Mush. "It took us four hours to the trapdoor from the castle. Let us see how long we are walking for so we can gauge how close we are to the castle and to Lilim." The tunnel was wide enough for three or four creatures to walk side by side. It was high enough for all of them to walk standing upright. The walls were dirt but seemed to be coated with something because you could not scrape any dirt off the walls. The floor was all dirt, very dry dirt. There was no light, except the lights they had brought with them. It was dark and quiet and eerie. They had walked straight, quietly and slowly, for four and a half hours. Then they came upon a turn to the left, away from Lilim.

"We are about a half an hour away from the castle," stated Mush.

Hugo responded, "Let us continue to keep track of the time so we can get an idea of where we end up. Let's take a break. I'm hungry."

"Agreed," said Mush.

As they ate, Emil chuckled. "We are below-below ground."

"Yes. What's so funny?" replied Mush.

"This is a tunnel created by your Fallen Brothers as an escape route. This has been here for some time. They must have known that someday you would find out what they were doing," said Emil.

"Yes," responded Mush again. "What's so funny?"

"I was laughing because I am below my world, and now we are below ground in your world. We are below-below ground."

Birdy began to laugh. "I get it, below-below ground."

Hugo, a little grumpy, said, "Birdy, go fly down the tunnel and see what's ahead. Everyone, finish up what you are eating. It's getting late, and we should continue and find a place to camp for the night." Birdy flew down the tunnel to see if there was anything he could see. Birdy could see a dim light not too far in the distance. Birdy flew back to the group. "There is a dim light not too far in the distance. It may be a way out."

"Let's clean up and continue forward," replied Mush. They gathered their things and headed toward the dim light. After walking for a half an hour, they came upon the dim light. It was a slit in the earth, like the other end of the tunnel.

"Mush," called Hugo. "You should go through the crack and see what is up there. We do not want to end up in the middle of our Fallen Brother's lair."

"Good idea," replied Mush, and with that, he mushed through the slit. Mush quickly blended into the earth to look around. He was on another path that continued to lead away from Lilim and the castle. Behind the trapdoor was a dense wooded area with the same briar bushes as on the path out of the castle. So there is only one way to go forward.

Mush mushed back under the slit of light in the door. "There is another path to follow right in front of the door. And a dense wooded area with briar bushes behind the door. It is just like at the other end but no grass or meadow. There are, however, some trees closer to the edge of the trail within the briar bushes."

Hugo responded, "It is late. We do not know what we will run into up there. So let us go back to the turn and make camp there. We can set up some sort of alarm in case we get company. We will continue our journey in the morning." They all looked at each other and agreed. They made their way back to the turn and set up camp and an alarm in case of company.

Chapter 19

Meanwhile, back in Lilim, Snailstein and Rooty sat down to go over all the evidence again. Shelly walked into the lab to see what the others were doing. Rooty talking to himself, "If I bring down an inanimate object and do not morph it, it comes down normal size for Lilim. If I bring down an inanimate object and do morph it, it comes down to the size it was up top. If I bring up an inanimate object and morph it, it gets smaller. If I bring up an inanimate object and do not morph it, it stays the same size. Yet with living things, we cannot pull them up without morphing them. We can make things our size but cannot make them bigger for the top world."

Shelly and Snailstein were listening intently. Snailstein, with his deep, distinguished voice, said, "There needs to be another way to get to the top world other than morphing. Maybe we do not go through the root system. Maybe we try to find another way to make it to the top world. Maybe we dig a tunnel to the top world."

Rooty, pondering this idea, scrunched his face and was quiet for a bit and then began, "How would that make the children back to their normal size? And what do we do about the scars on the roots in the root system?"

Snailstein, more determined now, said, "We can figure that out later. One thing at a time. Let us talk to Tall One and see what he thinks about trying to build a tunnel to the top world." Rooty nods and the two of them begin to walk out. Shelly, following them, said, "Maybe it doesn't matter. Maybe we become ourselves again and our own size once we get back to our world." As they all thought about this idea, they walked silently together to see Tall One.

As the trio walked up to Tall One, Snailstein broke the silence. "Tall One, we want to build a tunnel to the top world. We don't know if Emil and Shelly will become their own size up top, but this idea is sound. Also, it will give the root system a break while we find a way to heal the roots."

Tall One sat silent for a minute. "This endeavor will be a tough one. We need to find a place for all the dirt without letting our Fallen Brothers know that we are here. We must also figure out a way to keep the tunnel from collapsing on itself. Snailstein, you draw up a plan of how this can actually be accomplished. Meanwhile, Rooty will try and figure out a way to get the children back to their normal size once on the top world. Also figure out how to save the root system. Go draw up a plan and bring it to me by morning."

Snailstein and Rooty began to walk back to the lab. Shelly, following them, said, "I can help with that plan." As they walked, Rooty began to come up with some ideas. "We can build the tunnel next to one of the accesses to the root system. But not too close to home. We can dig next to the root and use that as one side of the tunnel." They all entered the lab still listening to Rooty. "We can then use our lighted path technology to encompass the tunnel as we dig."

Snailstein questioned, "How do we keep the dirt from falling on top of us? And where do we put the dirt?" The three of them sat thinking for a while. Shelly paced around the lab. Rooty rolled back and forth. Snailstein just sat still. Rooty stopped rolling and began, "Okay, we dig the tunnel on an angle toward the top world. This will keep the dirt from falling on us as we dig. We just need to find a root system that is not too close to home. Near an entrance root system and that goes up on an angle to the top world."

Snailstein, a little worried, said, "We still need to figure out where to put the dirt." He began talking out loud, "If we just pile it up, it will be noticed. We could spread it out over a long stretch of land but that would be a lot more work and we would probably get noticed. Oh, maybe we can make little mounds here and there to look like it belongs with the terrain. We can also use some of it to reinforce our back wall of the cave."

Rooty nodded. "You have your work cut out for you looking for the perfect spot. I will go search the root system and see what I can find and take a closer look at those scars. I will meet you at the café at dinner."

Rooty went to the root system to find a place to dig the tunnel. Rooty went the opposite way to the castle. Rooty found a root that led up to the top world on an angle. It was half an hour away from Lilim. The surrounding area had some woods, but not too dense, which left lots of area to place the dirt mounds. However, there was one small problem. This root was off another root and not close enough to the one which could access the use of the lighted technology. Once Rooty found a good spot for the tunnel, he took a closer look at the scars on the roots. First, he used some dirt to try and patch the roots, but to no avail. Rooty then tried to cover the scars with a cream he uses on scars on himself. This seemed to help heal the root, but this was just a temporary fix to the problem. Rooty headed back to the café for dinner.

At the café, Rooty found Snailstein, Shelly, and Tall One already eating. Rooty joined them. "I found a root a half an hour away, but we cannot use the lighted technology. There is plenty of room to put the dirt and make little mounds so that it looks like the terrain. I found a temporary fix for the scars. The cream that I use for myself. However, we still need a more permanent plan. I should go through the root system and use my cream on all the scars until we find a better solution. I will do so after dinner." They had all stopped eating, listening intently to what Rooty was saying. Tall One took a drink and then said, "Good. We will begin first thing in the morning. We will dig in small groups so we can continue to dig and rotate as necessary as not to get tired out and to get it done. Rooty, you can go tomorrow throughout the root system and begin to heal the roots. Then you and Snailstein will have to replicate the lighted technology for the new tunnel. So make a list of small groups and get to it first thing in the morning."

Chapter 20

As they began to settle in to sleep, Mush decided to take the first watch. Almost as soon as the rest of them laid down, they heard the alarm that they had set up. Mush said, "Quickly, Emil and Hugo, come here into this little dented section of the underground wall. Brothers, mush up and cover them so they cannot be seen, and Birdy fly over head out of sight." Mush and the Mush brothers mushed, looking like the underground path walls and stood in front of Emil and Hugo just in time.

Then they heard *tad-thump*, *tad-thump*, *tad-thump* getting closer and the stench of foul drool. Elephant Man slowly passed them with a cart drawn behind him. The cart was empty. *Tad-thump, tad-thump, tad-thump*, he was gone out of sight. Mush and his brothers "unmushed" as Emil and Hugo stepped out. Birdy landed on the ground.

Hugo began, "If he's going back to the castle, it will take a while to get back. So we can sleep in shifts. We must also set up an alarm the other way in case he does come back." They all agreed. Once again, they settled down to sleep. Morning came, and they had a small snack for breakfast.

Hugo said, "We slept for about six hours. It takes about five hours to get to the castle and five hours to get back. We've been here for another two hours. So if Elephant Man is to come back through, we have two hours before he gets here. So do we stay here and hide like before, or do we forge forth and hope we can hide somewhere up there?"

Mush jumped in, "We should forge ahead. We have two hours on him, and we do not know how far we have yet to travel." They all agreed and gathered their belongings and once again began their journey down a path they didn't know. They slowly opened the door. Mush mushed out first to make sure that no one was there. "It's safe," called Mush. They all then slowly came out of the tunnel to continue their journey.

After walking for another half an hour, they came upon an abandoned cart with cages on it. "Stay here while Hugo and I go explore up ahead," said Mush. Emil, Birdy, and the Mush brothers went back a little way and found a place to hide off the path. Hugo and Mush slowly crept around the cart. There they saw a compound surrounded by high castle walls. Hugo waited behind the cart while Mush slowly crept to the wall. He found the entrance and mushed himself into a slit by the entrance gate. Mush could see lots of Fallen Brothers walking around with weapons. There was a big castle in the distance, but not like the other castle. This was much bigger. It actually looked like a castle.

Mush mushed back and told Hugo what he had seen. The two of them went back to the others. As they got to the others, they heard *tad-thump, tad-thump, tad-thump* of the Elephant Man return-ing. Quickly, they all did as they had done before, but now in the woods, it was easier to hide. *Tad-thump, tad-thump, tad-thump* came Elephant Man, but this time, he did not have a cart with him. *Tad-thump, tad-thump, tad-thump*, he passed. Mush and his brothers fol-lowed slowly behind to get a better look at the compound.

Mush and his brothers dodged out of the way of the falling foul drool of the Elephant Man, following closely behind so as not to be seen. Once at the gate, it opened without hesitation. *They must have been expecting Elephant Man*, thought Mush to himself. Mush and his brothers mushed into the dirt and slithered behind Elephant Man all the way to the castle.

The castle was surrounded by guards on each side of the entrance. Mush motioned to his brothers to follow him around the side of the castle and away from his Fallen Brothers. They went around the side and found a place on the side to "unmush" and talk. "We need to find another way in to see what our brothers are up to," said Mush.

Mushy responded, "I will go back to the others and let them know what you two are up to. I will take them back to the tunnel and wait there."

"Good," replied Mush. "Musher and I will find a way into the castle and see what is going on. We will meet you back at the tunnel in two hours. If we are not back in three hours, go back to Lilim and let Tall One know what is going on. Go now!"

Mush and his brother mushed back into the earth and went farther around the castle until they found a way in through what seemed to be a kitchen. It was an open doorway with no visible door. They both peered around the corner and saw no one. Slowly, they went inside. There they hid under a table leg and looked around. It was a huge area. They were under a table. Around the outside walls were counters. The counters were full of cooking items and buckets of food. Above the counters were cabinets. There was one way out of the kitchen and into the castle. From under the table, they could see a corridor going into the castle. The corridor wound around to the left. "How are we going to find stuff in here?" asked Musher.

"We will split up," stated Mush. "I will find out where Elephant Man went, and you find out what you can going the opposite way. We will meet back here in one and a half hours."

Mush went out of the kitchen area and found the path of foul drool. It led up a few stairs and into a dining area. There in front of Mush was Elephant Man, Coily, and Gator. Gator was a smaller creature. He was slender with a big, long jaw and lots of pointy teeth. *Gator may be small, but he is the leader of our Fallen Brothers and could lead us to the truth about the children*, thought Mush.

Mush slowly crept toward the table to hear what they were saying. Mush paused as Coily dropped something and bent down to pick it up. He did not see Mush. Mush was relieved and again began to creep closer and very slowly to hear them. Mush finally got right under one of the table legs near Gator. He stood quietly, hiding behind the table leg.

"There was no sign of anyone following me," stated Elephant Man.

"Let's give it another day or two before we go back to the castle," replied Gator. "And we should start the process with the new children as soon as possible."

In response, Coily stated, "I will get right on that, but what of the two children that we lost? Was there any sign of them? They couldn't have just disappeared."

Elephant Man said, "I looked everywhere and found nothing. It's like I said, our Light Brother seized them. They must live somewhere close to the root system where I lost them." As the two of them began to argue back and forth, Mush slowly went back to meet up with his brother Musher.

"Stop arguing!" demanded Gator. "We have to send out a search party to find the children. Elephant Man, get a team together and go. Coily, begin the process with the children and have them start working right away. We need more people helping gather food from our crops." Elephant Man and Coily left. Gator got up and exited the room, which had a balcony where Gator could see his entire kingdom from.

Meanwhile, Musher had gone around the castle looking in the rooms in order to find all the children. But there was no one in sight. Musher had found a window to the courtyard of the castle, and there were lots of children. They were cleaning the grounds, delivering food, or doing other jobs while the Fallen Brothers were lounging around or wandering around with weapons like guards. It was odd because none of the children seemed to be old. They were all young, like ten to thirteen years old. No older children were seen. Musher scratched his head and decided to return to the kitchen to meet up with Mush.

Mush arrived in the kitchen area before Musher did. Mush saw a young girl beginning to peel potatoes. Mush crept slowly around to see if there was anyone else nearby. As Mush got to the corner where he was to meet Musher, he heard Coily. "You need to peel faster." He laughed as he passed the girl. The young girl shrugged away as Coily touched the girl's hair. Coily continued on his way. Mush saw his brother and waved to him to stop and wait. Musher stopped but tapped his arm for time. Mush nodded and waived Musher toward him. They both crept back to the castle gate before saying a word. Once at the gate, Mush began, "I saw Gator. He is in the castle. Elephant Man is putting a team together to try and find us. Coily is going to get the new children processed in order to start work right away. But I am not sure exactly what Gator meant by that."

Musher responded, "I saw a bunch of the children in the court-yard cleaning the grounds, delivering food. Our Fallen Brothers have enslaved all the children while they just sit around and do nothing. None of the children are older than thirteen years. What do you think that means?"

Mush and Musher arrived at the tunnel in the time that they had given the others. Once in the tunnel, they explained what they had found. "We need to go back to Lilim and speak to Tall One. We need to leave before Elephant Man comes back with his crew," stated Mush. Without a word, they all packed up and went back the way they had come. They were careful not to leave any trace of them-selves. When they got to the beginning of the tunnel, they decided to stop for the night and camp in the tunnel for safe cover. They would start at first light and be home by lunch.

Chapter 21

Rooty set up groups to start digging the tunnel. Rooty oversaw the start of the dig. "Remember to dig next to the root, but not too close. We do not want to damage the actual root." Rooty decided that the elders would start the tunnel. Once they got a little ways in, the children would begin. They would take a shovel and a bunch of pails and do a dirt brigade. One of the creatures would shovel dirt and fill a pail. That pail would be passed to another creature until it reached a wheelbarrow and then the dirt would be dumped. Then one creature would run the pail back to the beginning where the process could start all over. As some of the creatures of Lilim began to dig, others wheeled the dirt away and began making little mounds. It had to look like the terrain had always been there.

Shelly watched as they dug shovelful after shovelful of dirt and hauled it away. "How are you going to light up the tunnel if you do not have access to the root system?" asked Shelly.

Snailstein, who was closely inspecting the tunnel with each shovelful of dirt, replied, "I am not sure, but we will figure it out. First things first."

"What does that mean?" asked Shelly.

"It means we dig the tunnel, and as we get farther to the surface, someone will come up with an idea. You worry too much. All will be as it should be," stated Snailstein in his deep, distinguished voice.

This went on late into the evening with everyone taking turns so as not to tire out. Tall One arrived and stopped everyone. "Get some rest. We can resume in the morning after a good night's sleep. Head over to the café and get something to eat." The tunnel seemed to be really long, but also very narrow. Tall One thought they would widen it next. He was pleased with the progress and smiled as he walked into the café with Snailstein.

Tall One asked, "How stable is the tunnel? And how will it stay stable as we widen it?"

Snailstein replied, "I will have to use some of our technology from Rooty to make it like the tunnels of the root system. But how to strengthen it to go upward, I am not sure."

Shelly was walking slowly behind them. She was listening to them intently as they talked about the tunnel. Shelly walked up beside them and began, "You can start building the tunnel with steps so that it isn't too steep and then maybe your technology will work."

Snailstein looked puzzled but responded, "That is a good idea, but how do we make the tunnel steps? Oh, we will have to dig ahead and slowly come in behind making steps. This will take longer to build the tunnel, but it will be safer and easier to use."

Tall One looked at them both. "Good. Then it's settled. Have something to eat, and we can get a fresh start in the morning."

Shelly got her food and sat by herself on the hill by the river. She wondered if Emil and the others were okay and when they would be back. Shelly thought that helping with the tunnel would take her mind off not being home or wondering what her family and Emil's family were thinking. One of the children of Lilim walked over to Shelly and whispered, "I know what you are doing."

Shelly, startled, replied, "How do you know that I was thinking of home and if Emil is safe?"

The child replied, "You just told me." With that they both laughed.

Early the next morning, Rooty was at the tunnel inspecting all that was done and all that needed to be done and where to start. Soon the elders and the children arrived. Rooty began by letting them know how to widen the tunnel. Snailstein arrived with Shelly. "We have to build it in steps as we go up once it is widened. This way it will not collapse as we walk up it."

Rooty responded, "The elders will begin to widen the tunnel, and Snailstein and I will come up with a way to build the steps within the tunnel. The children will continue to spread the dirt and make mounds to make it look natural." No one responded. They just got to work without a word.

Shelly sat with Rooty and Snailstein and came up with a way to build the steps within the tunnel. Rooty said, "Now with that done, I have to come up with a way to use our technology to light up the tunnel to use the root next to it without damaging our root system. You two continue watching over the dig, and I will go to my original root system plans and see if I can come up with a few ideas." Without another word, Rooty went back to his home. Shelly began to help the others while Snailstein continued to oversee the work.

Chapter 22

Birdy awoke to the others grumbling about Emil. "We have to find him. Where do you think he is?" muttered Mush.

"He couldn't have gotten far," replied Musher. They all headed toward the other end of the tunnel, bringing everything with them. They got to the other end of the tunnel, but there was no sight of Emil anywhere.

Emil, while on watch, crept up the tunnel and out of the tunnel. He then crept up the path to the castle of the Fallen Brothers. Emil crept around the outside of the walls to the castle, under bushes, trying to find a way in. Emil knew he had to stay hidden. Emil was covered in pickers and dirt, but he pushed on until he was too tired to move. Emil found a small bush and tucked himself under it and fell asleep.

As the sun rose, Emil, forgetting where he was, stretched and yawned and hit his arms on the main trunk of the bush. "Ouch!" exclaimed Emil. Realizing that he spoke out loud and remembering where he was, Emil looked around to see if anyone had heard him. No one came, so Emil crawled under bushes by the wall once again and continued his journey to find a way into the castle.

Emil came upon a small crack in the wall. He peered through the crack and saw a few children picking what looked like apples from a tree. However, the apples were purple in color. One of the children saw Emil looking through the crack in the wall. The child's eyes grew wide and began to tear. But he did not say a word. Emil, knowing that the boy saw him, waved to the boy. The boy just slowly shook his head. Emil looked at all the other children, but they were just diligently picking the apples, not paying any attention to anything else. Soon, one of the guards came by, and the boy who was staring at Emil slowly turned back to pick apples as if he had never seen Emil. The guard looked at each of the children's baskets. If he was pleased with what the children had picked for the morning, he would give them food. If the basket wasn't full enough, he would pass them by and go onto the next child. Once he saw all the children's baskets, he went back the way he had come. With none of the children paying attention to Emil, he stopped looking.

Emil decided to continue looking for a way in. Emil walked farther down the wall. Emil then heard a noise, so he slowly crept along the wall so as not to be seen. Emil had come to a river. There was no more wall. *Could this be a way into the castle?* Emil thought. This was a river that was a lot bigger than the stream he was used to playing in and crossing with Shelly. Emil stared wide eyed, thinking of how he could cross the river. Emil looked around, but there were no logs to cross. There were no big trees on this side of the river. Emil, looking at the river, thought out loud, "What to do…do I go back to the tunnel and get the others? Or do I try to swim across the river? No. No, it's going way too fast. Or do I just wait here?"

Meanwhile, Birdy, Hugo, and the Mush brothers were in search of Emil. They quickly got to the entrance of the castle of their Fallen Brothers. Mush and his brothers quickly found Emil's path and cleaned up his tracks as they went forward to find him. Birdy asked, "Why are you covering Emil's tracks? What if he needs to find his way back?"

Mush answered, "If we do not cover his tracks, and our Fallen Brothers find him, then we have a bigger problem than Emil being lost. Also, we are following his tracks and should find him first."

Birdy looked a little calmer and helped the Mush brothers cover the tracks and follow the trail.

While Emil was looking around at the river deciding what to do, Birdy, Hugo, and the Mush brothers were getting closer and closer to Emil. Just then, in front of Emil, one of the Fallen Brothers emerged from the water. He was shaped like a shell with one big eye on top. He had one leg coming out of either side of the shell. Each leg had a claw at the end. He had sharp jagged teeth and snarled at Emil. Emil tried to back away, but in an instance, he was grabbed up by the claws of Cycrabster. He was swooped into the river and across to the other side before Emil could even take a breath. Birdy, Hugo, and the Mush brothers got to the river just as Cycrabster swooped up Emil. They were all stunned and just sat there wondering what they should do next.

Cycrabster took Emil to see Gator. Emil found himself standing next to a big table in a big dining hall with Gator sitting at the head

of the table. Emil was dripping wet but so in awe of the castle and everything in it. Emil forgot that he was not home, that he was in danger, and these wonderous creatures were not his friends.

Gator asked, "What is your name, boy?" No response. So again, Gator asked, "What is your name, boy? Where did you come from? Are you one of the children that my men lost to the Light Brothers?" Still no response. Gator looked at Cycrabster who responded, "I found him on the other side of the river. I saw the Mush brothers as I swooped into the river."

Gator, a little taken back, said, "So our brothers have found us. They could not have gone far. Take this one to the yard and tie him up until he talks. Then go get Elephant Man and send him to me."

"Yes, right away!" replied Cycrabster. And off he went with Emil, who was still looking at everything and not really noticing anything.

Cycrabster took Emil out of the castle and tied him up. Emil was tied up in the middle of the square for everyone to see. Emil, now snapping out of his trance-like state, seemed shaken up. Emil looked around for a friendly face, but all he saw was Fallen Brothers and children who paid no attention to him. Emil began to panic and tried to pull out of the ropes. "Help me!" Emil cried. No one ever looked his way. "Why don't you help me?" questioned Emil but still no one looked his way. Emil continued to try and get out of the ropes, but to no avail.

Mush told Birdy to fly to the tunnel and stay hidden until the Mush brothers and Hugo could get there. They needed to get back to Lilim and let Tall One and the others know about the Fallen Brothers capturing Emil. Birdy flew to the tunnel and hid in the bushes nearby. Birdy smelled the foul drool of the Elephant Man as he emerged from the tunnel and walked right by Birdy. Birdy nearly got hit by the foul-smelling drool as Elephant Man looked from side to side, as if searching for something. As Elephant Man passed, the Mush brothers and Hugo emerged out of the bushes nearby, and along with Birdy, they headed to the tunnel on their way back to Lilim.

In the big hall, Elephant Man sat with Gator. "I found no one on the road back to the castle and no sign of the Light Brothers," stated Elephant Man.

"I know," began Gator. "Mush and his brothers along with Hugo were spotted by the river, and Cycrabster caught one of the children that our Light Brothers were holding. I want you to take Coily and Cycrabster and find our Light Brothers. I will keep the boy and get whatever information I can out of him. Don't come back without any news."

As night fell, Emil was given water and bread by one of the Fallen Brothers. Still, no one spoke to him. The other children all avoided him and walked past as if he weren't there. Emil spotted the boy who he had seen picking purple apples. The boy did not respond to Emil but looked up once at him. Emil knew that the boy had noticed him and understood that he would not talk to him. The boy just walked with the other children. They went to the back of the castle and down into the dungeon. There were cots lined up in rows for all the children to sleep.

The boy sat on his cot, and when the others laid down, the boy slowly crept out of the dungeon. He walked slowly and quietly sneaking past the one guard who never really watched the dungeon door. This guard was shaped like a U. He had two skinny arms with five fingers on each hand. He had two legs, but his feet had no toes. His eyes were on either side of his face, which was at the top of the U-shaped body. His mouth was at the bottom of his U-shaped body. He had two horns at the top of his head, one on either side of his U-shaped body. Right above each eye. His tongue was forked at the end and long, like a snake's tongue. He stood and watched the other direction while doing pull ups on a bar that was fixed to the wall.

The boy walked around the trees to the other side of Emil, where no one could see him. "Hi, my name is George," said the boy quietly.

"My name is Emil," responded Emil softly.

George began, "They will condition you not to do anything but what you are asked to do or you will get tortured. We all have been here for some time and just go about our day. I don't have a lot of time, so how did you get here?"

Emil quietly replied, "I am with the Light Brothers. We came to see what the Fallen Brothers were up to, and when I heard about all you children like me, I had to find out more. I know that the Light Brothers will come for us."

George, while walking away, said, "I have to go. I hope that there is someone out there who can help us." George went back to the dungeon and went to sleep. Emil sat quietly and tried to sleep. Emil was finding it hard to get settled being tied up, but he soon dozed off.

Chapter 23

Birdy, Hugo, and the Mush brothers made it back to Lilim by lunch time. Most of Lilim was gathered at the café, except the group that was still working in the tunnel. Tall One and Shelly greeted Birdy, Hugo, and the Mush brothers as they entered the café. Shelly, puzzled, asked, "Where is Emil? Did he stop at the tunnel to see how things are going?"

Mush looked at Tall One and slowly began, "We encountered our Fallen Brothers. We were on our way back to let you know where they were and what they were up to. Last night, Emil was on guard duty. He snuck out and then got captured by our Fallen Brothers." A gasp was let out throughout the café. Mush continued, "When Emil got captured by Cycrabster, we were seen. We need to step up our defenses. They will be searching for us and Shelly. We also need to come up with a plan to save Emil and help him escape. They have a lot of children."

Tall One nodded in agreement. He began, "We are still working on the tunnel. We have a good idea where it will end up. We still need Rooty to incorporate our lighted technology for the children. But we believe that the tunnel will be done within two days. Also, we must come up with a way to hide the tunnel. We do not need our Fallen Brothers finding it." After some silence, Tall One began again, "Let us get another group down to the tunnel. Let's get Rooty and Snailstein up here so you can go over the entire mission."

Birdy, Hugo, and the Mush brothers got something to eat and cleaned up. Shelly and Tall One went to the tunnel. They told Rooty and Snailstein about what had happened to Emil and who the team had run into. Once the new group was set up in the tunnel and knew what needed to be done, everyone else went back to the café.

Once at the café, Mush began telling everyone about the hidden tunnel, then the castle and where Emil was being held captive. He also talked about which of the Fallen Brothers were at the castle. As soon as Tall One heard that Gator, Cycrabster, and Coily were all together, he responded, "We must tighten our defenses immediately! Put a group of three on watch near the cave entrance. Also put a detail of guards at the tunnel that we are building right away. Snailstein and Rooty, your first priority will be to figure out a way we can hide the tunnel from others. So if our Fallen Brothers come, we need a place for our workers to hide."

As soon as Tall One finished, Snailstein and Rooty left for the tunnel. Tall One then continued, "Mush, you, Hugo, and the Mush brothers need to come up with a plan to get Emil back. Birdy, fly to the first castle and then come warn us when you see our Fallen Brothers arrive. Shelly, you should stay here where it is safe."

Shelly replied. "I mean no disrespect, but I need to do something to help. I will not go with the group to save Emil, but I would like to listen to the plan and help where I can."

Tall One looked at Shelly. "You can help with the plan, but you must stay here. We are already missing Emil and who knows how many more children our Fallen Brothers have." Hugo, Shelly, Mush, and his brothers sat at a table at the café. Everyone else, including Tall One, left. "It takes a total of five and a half hours to get to the main castle," started Hugo.

Chapter 24

Snailstein and Rooty were back at the lab, looking over their notes. Snailstein looked at Rooty with a puzzled look. Then, in his deep, distinguished voice, he said, "If it takes four hours to get to the tunnel, and they traveled a half hour back and then a half hour to the exit and a half hour to the castle, the big castle should be two hours due east and a half hour due south of Lilim."

Rooty looked at Snailstein. "You should let the others know and see if this will help. Maybe they won't have to take the long way. I will go back to the tunnel and keep on working on hiding the tunnel."

Snailstein went to Hugo's Café and Grill and let Hugo and the others know about the castle. Hugo looked at Shelly and the Mush brothers. "We should send One Arm to take over for Birdy. Shelly, go let Tall One know what's going on, and Mush, you and I will talk to Birdy."

As soon as Hugo finished, Birdy appeared. "One Arm sent me."

Hugo replied, "One Arm must have heard us. Birdy, if you fly south for half an hour and east two hours, you should be at the big castle. Fly and let us know if it is passable that way and if we can get there without our Fallen Brothers knowing."

Birdy flew off without saying a word. Birdy flew southeast. As Birdy flew, he could see the sea far in the distance toward the south. Birdy did not see a clear path for his brothers to follow, but they could create a path through the woods. As Birdy neared the castle, he could see the raging river where Emil was taken. It was just a short distance from Lilim. Birdy could not see a clear way into the Fallen Brother's castle other than over the raging river. No one was watching the river.

Birdy spotted a crack in the wall that Emil must have passed. Birdy fluttered in front of the crack to see if it was safe to fly over the wall. Birdy saw trees with purple fruit hanging from them. The children were picking fruit from those trees but no guards. Birdy flew over the wall and landed in one of the trees way up high. Birdy could see the entire field and lots of children working. Birdy did not see Emil. He was too far away from the castle. Birdy flew to a tree that was closer to the castle. From there, he could see Emil in the center of the square. There were guards all around the castle. Birdy could not get any closer but could see that Emil was still alive. Birdy flew back to the other tree and still no guards near the children. Birdy flew back over the wall. He landed in a nearby tree and looked around. Birdy looked northwest. Although most of it was covered with briar bushes, there were some spaces that had other bushes, and Birdy thought it would be a good way to get to the castle in less time. Birdy flew back to Lilim.

Birdy met with Tall One and the others. Birdy said, "I saw Emil and he is still alive. There is no good way into the castle other than over the raging river. I found a place through the trees that we could make our own path in order to get to the castle sooner."

Tall One responded, "This is good news. Now we can come up with a plan to save Emil. We can also make this new path through the woods so we can get there quicker. Maybe our Fallen Brothers will be unaware of us, and we can have the upper hand.

Evening came and the café was quiet. Only a few creatures here and there. Tall One first checked the cave and its defenses. Tall One walked all over Lilim and checked the cave entrance. Once Tall One was good with everything that was done for protection, he made his way to the tunnel.

At the tunnel, it seemed as if there was no one there except the four guards. Tall One asked, "Where is the tunnel? You covered it well." One of the guards pointed to a small mound of dirt. Tall One went to the mound of dirt and looked at it. All he saw was dirt. Tall One looked back at the guard and then back at the mound of dirt. This time, there was an open door. It was camouflaged so well, it only looked like a mound of dirt.

Tall One had to duck to get into the tunnel. Once inside the tunnel, all Tall One could see was steps going up and up. It was dark up there. Just then, Rooty came down the steps and was visible.

"How far up does it go?" asked Tall One.

"We are almost there, I think. I stopped calculating to finish hiding the cave entrance. Now all we have to do is come up with a way to get our lighted technology into the tunnel from the root system," replied Rooty.

Tall One responded, "You did a great job hiding the tunnel and its entrance. Birdy found a shorter way to the castle. Our defenses are solid. Mush and Hugo will come up with a plan. You will figure out the lighting, and everything else will fall into place."

Chapter 25

lephant Man, Coily, and Cycrabster took off through the tunnel and back to the first castle. Upon entering the castle, Coily stated, "Once again, it feels like home, and you did a good job fixing it up."

Elephant Man replied, "I only had a little time before I was called back. We must look for the Light Brothers and find them." They looked at each other and then walked out of the castle and around to the front gate where Coily stood guard. Elephant Man looked up and down the path. "I think we should go this way," he said pointing to his right.

"Why?" asked Cycrabster.

"We have been up this way, and this is where I lost the boy to our Light Brothers. I can show you where I found him in the root system." Cycrabster and Coily nodded. The Fallen Brothers headed up the path. *Tad-thump, tad-thump, tad-thump* down the path went Elephant Man leaving drips of foul-smelling drool.

As they neared the root system, Cycrabster asked, "Have you ever ventured down this path?" It was a steep cliff leading down toward ferns.

"No," replied Elephant Man, "I go up to the root system and jump into the roots from there. And go wherever I need." Cycrabster looked down the steep cliff. "Maybe we should try this one first." Coily looked down the cliff. "I don't think so. Elephant Man will tumble, and I'm not carrying him back up."

Cycrabster laughed and the three of them headed to the root system. *Tad-thump, tad-thump, tad-thump* was heard as they went into the lighted area of the root system. Elephant Man walked them down the path and explained what he had done and seen. The three of them walked the path and then back to the lit area. "Where do you think they went from here?" asked Cycrabster.

"This is as far as I travel. Then I go into the root system and pick up children from there," replied Elephant Man. Cycrabster looked around. "I think that we should head back up top and take one of the other paths. Our Light Brothers have to be nearby.

They went out of the root system and back to where the path split. The path that either leads back to the castle or down the steep cliff. Coily looked around and saw a path a little farther past the root system. "Let's try that way." Coily pointed toward the path. "It looks like a good idea to me," responded Cycrabster.

They walked down the path and found little mounds of dirt in a barren area. "This looks very dry," stated Cycrabster. They all laughed and continued on. Elephant Man went first. *Tad-thump, tad-thump, tad-thump* as he walked. They walked around the mounds of dirt, which went on for what seemed like miles. *Tad-thump, tad-thump, tad-thump.* All the while drips of foul drool fell from Elephant Man, sizzling the dirt, splashing on the sides of the mounds of dirt. The foul smell drifted into the air and into the tunnel. The tunnel was hidden, and the Fallen Brothers were close, but the odor drifted up the shaft of the tunnel.

Coily called, "Slow down, Elephant Man. There is nothing here for miles. We should have taken the other path."

Cycrabster answered, "I think we should continue. We have a hidden tunnel. Maybe they do also."

Elephant Man continued walking—*tad-thump, tad-thump, tad-thump*. He did not look back or slow down. He just continued on— *tad-thump, tad-thump, tad-thump, tad-thump*.

"Hold on," cried Elephant Man. "I think I found something. These mounds of dirt are getting bigger. I would say that they have been altered or something is hidden in one of them." Coily and Cycrabster caught up and looked at all the mounds of dirt. They saw that they were bigger than the ones they had just passed.

Coily asked, "What are we looking for? Where do we begin? They are all bigger, but they all still look the same." Elephant Man turned suddenly. "I have been listening to the sound of the sizzle of my drool. When the dirt is softer, as if it had been recently dug up, they drool will seep into the earth and sound less."

"What does that mean?" questioned Coily, puzzled. Elephant Man began to walk again. "It means less sizzle sound." *Tad-thump, tad-thump, tad-thump, tad-thump.* "Like here. I hear less sizzle."

Cycrabster, without a word, began digging in that spot. "Nothing," stated Cycrabster.

"Less sizzle here," responded Elephant Man. Once again, Cycrabster began digging. And once again, Elephant Man continued to walk. *Tad-thump, tad-thump, tad-thump.*

"Less sizzle here," called Elephant Man once again. Cycrabster was still digging at the last spot, so Coily began digging this spot.

"Nothing," called Cycrabster.

"Nothing," called Coily. "I don't think this is working."

"Give it a little more time. We just started." replied Cycrabster.

"Less sizzle here" was once again heard from Elephant Man. This continued for several hours. "Less sizzle here," called Elephant Man. Coily looked back. "I think we may have made a mistake."

"What do you mean?" asked Cycrabster.

"I mean, look at all the dirt piles that we just dug up. And then piled up again. They look different from the ones we dug and different from the smaller ones in the beginning. Maybe their lair is hidden in the smaller ones," Coily stated.

Cycrabster nodded and said, "Elephant Man, come back." *Tad-thump.*

"Less sizzle here," called Elephant Man.

Cycrabster, louder now, said, "Come back, Elephant Man. I think that you are right, Coily. The Light Brothers would not travel so far away from the root system." Without another word, they began to walk back to the smaller mounds of dirt.

Once at the smaller mounds of dirt, Elephant Man called, "Less sizzle here." Once again, Cycrabster began to dig, still finding nothing.

"Less sizzle here," called Elephant Man. And once again, Coily began digging, still finding nothing. After several hours of digging up the smaller mounds, Cycrabster stated, "We have been digging all day. Maybe we should go back to the split in the path and take the steep trail to try and find our Light Brothers."

Elephant Man replied, "Maybe they are not underground. Maybe we should go back to the split in the path."

Coily commented, "We will go back to the split path. But we must continue to think of other places that our Light Brothers would be. We will search that trail first." The three of them began their way back to the split in the trail. *Tad-thump, tad-thump, tad-thump.*

Chapter 26

One Arm appeared at the café. "Our Fallen Brothers are at the castle and will soon be coming our way to look for us."

"Who was with them?" asked Tall One.

One Arm replied, "Cycrabster, Coily, and Elephant Man."

Tall One spoke, "We all knew that this day would come. We knew when we found Emil and Shelly that our lives had been changed. Everyone knows their role and what they need to do. We will continue to do what we must to protect ourselves and our friends." It was quiet while Tall One spoke. As soon as he was done, everyone went right back to what they were doing without hesitation.

Tad-thump, tad-thump, tad-thump was heard, and the odorous smell of the foul stench of Elephant Man was strong in the cave. No one panicked. Everyone just went to their posts without anyone giving directions. Everyone knew their jobs and just went about as if it were just another day.

In the tunnel, you could smell the foul drool of Elephant Man as it went into the ground and up the tunnel shaft. Rooty quietly called to his coworkers, "We must finish the tunnel and get to the top world. So let us continue quietly. We are almost at the top world, and next, we will have to find a solution for lighting the tunnel. The odor is outside, and our tunnel is well hidden." No one stopped as Rooty talked; they just listened as they worked.

Hugo and Mush were talking about ways to get into the castle and to get Emil back. Hugo looked at Mush and began, "We are going about this all wrong. We need to go simple. We can do what we did when we passed Coily. You and the Mush brothers can get in leaves, and I will blow you passed the guards and through the gate. The three of you can roll as far as I can blow you. Then mush into the ground until you have a safe path to safety or Emil."

Mush looked at Hugo. "That is a great idea. Go simple. I know that we can get to Emil with all of what Birdy told us. But how do we then get Emil out?"

Hugo responded, "It has to be fast. They can't see it coming. We will have to set up a diversion."

Mush, still thinking, said, "How many others are we going to try and get out? How do we get Emil out of the shackles? And how do we get back without being followed?"

Hugo now looking puzzled. "We will have to ask Tall One his expectations, but we have to move fast. Our Fallen Brothers are upon us."

Mush approached Tall One as he finished his speech. "We need to have some clarification in order to move forward on our plan to save Emil. How many others do you want us to rescue? How fast can we get them without being followed? And where do you want us to lead them to?"

Tall One stood quiet for a moment. "You need to get Emil out. If you can get any others without jeopardizing our goal, then get more out. Before you start, we will make sure that the tunnel is ready. You will take them directly to the tunnel, and they will go to the top world immediately."

Hugo, listening intently, said, "What if the tunnel is done, but the children cannot get to the top world?"

Tall One replied, "If it does not work, then we will bring the children back to Lilim and go from there. Now go finish your plan, and I will make sure that the tunnel is ready. Meet me here when the plan is done."

Mush and Hugo went back to the lab to finalize their plan. On the way, they picked up Birdy to get some more information. Hugo asked, "How much of a path do we have to create to go the short way to the castle of our Fallen Brothers?"

Birdy began, "You don't really have to make a path. You just need to have the children, and of course, you, Hugo, crawl under the smaller bushes. Then there will be a path for our Fallen Brothers to follow."

"Okay, we will get back to that problem in a bit," replied Hugo. "Now what type of diversion can we make to get the children out and not have all our Fallen Brothers on our tails?"

Mush responded, "We should create the diversion near the river. This will send our Fallen Brothers in the opposite direction of where we need to be."

Birdy then said, "Most of the children will be in the fields near the river."

Hugo replied, "We can only save who we can, and Emil is our priority. Birdy, you can be our diversion. You can make yourself be seen and give us time to get Emil free. And get Emil to the path without being seen or maybe even followed by our Fallen Brothers. Then you can fly away in a different direction to keep them going the wrong way. Let us go see Tall One with the details of our plan."

Once Tall One heard the plan, he responded, "Hugo, Mush, and your brothers, along with Birdy, will go and free Emil and any other children if possible. We will get Shelly to the tunnel. Once you have Emil, bring him straight to the tunnel so that the two of them and any other children can go home. Go now, while you have a chance."

Hugo, Birdy, Mush, and his brothers set out to the castle of their Fallen Brothers. They could smell the foul drool of Elephant Man and could hear *tad-thump, tad-thump, tad-thump* in the distance but getting closer. They hurried toward the sound and then quickly ducked into and under the bushes. Now *tad-thump, tad-*

thump, tad-thump was nearly on them. They made their way deeper into the woods.

After Hugo and his group left, Tall One looked at Shelly. "Once our Fallen Brothers have passed us, no matter what direction they go, we must get you to the tunnel. We must make sure that the tunnel is ready, and everything is set for you and Emil to go home." The stench of the foul drool was getting more potent. The eerie sounds and rumbling earth of *tad-thump, tad-thump, tad-thump* was getting closer and was nearly upon them. *Tad-thump, tad-thump, tad-thump* was getting louder. *Tad-thump, tad-thump, tad-thump* was now pounding at the cave entrance. *Tad-thump,* it stopped right in front of the cave entrance. There was silence in Lilim. Everyone was prepared for the worst. No one moved. They quietly prepared themselves for anything. Then *tad-thump, tad-thump, tad-thump, tad-thump* slowly got softer and softer.

Tall One said, "We must go now to the tunnel while our Fallen Brothers have passed."

Tall One, Shelly, and Snailstein made their way out of the cave and back to the tunnel. On their way, they saw the mounds of dirt were disturbed and dug into. The lingering foul odor of Elephant Man was present everywhere.

Rooty greeted them, "We heard our Fallen Brothers not too long ago."

Tall One replied, "Yes, they have just come down the cliff and passed the entrance to Lilim and kept going. Hugo, Birdy, Mush, and his brothers are on a rescue mission for Emil. Once they get Emil and any others, if possible, they will bring them here. The tunnel must be ready."

Rooty looked at Tall One. "We are just getting the lighting set up. It will be ready for them when they arrive."

Chapter 27

Cycrabster, Coily, and Elephant Man made their way to the split in the trail. Cycrabster looked down the steep cliff. "We will try this way,"

"Okay, but I should go first. If I fall, you will be knocked down in my path as I roll along." Elephant Man replied.

Cycrabster laughed, "Okay, you will go first."

Slowly, Elephant Man, Coily, and Cycrabster began down the steep cliff. *Tad-thump, tad-thump, tad-thump.* Elephant Man called to the others, "This is not a steep cliff, just a trail. I bet our Light Brothers live down this path."

Tad-thump, tad-thump, tad-thump. Then *tad-thump* and Elephant Man just stopped in front of the mushroom patch. He looked around. Not sensing anything, he waited for his brothers to catch up to him and continued down the path. Cycrabster looked farther down the path. "It looks like this winds up in the river. It does not look as if we can get anywhere from here unless we follow the river."

Coily responded, "Let's go to the end of the path and see what's there. If there is nothing, we will make our way back up the cliff and go from there." Without a word, the three of them continued on. *Tad-thump, tad-thump, tad-thump.* They finally got to the end of the trail, and there was the river.

"No place else to go," stated Cycrabster as he dove into the river. Cycrabster disappeared into the river. Coily looked at Elephant Man. "Now we wait." They waited for a while, and then Cycrabster popped up out of the water and back onto land right in front of Coily.

"Did you find anything?" asked Coily.

Cycrabster replied, "No, nothing in the water. No caves. No place for them to hide. We have to go back up the cliff and see what we missed. If we get to the top and find nothing, we should go back to Gator and let him know. Agreed?"

Both Coily and Elephant Man replied at the same time, "Agreed." The three of them began their journey up the cliff, but this time looking even more intently under every bush. *Tad-thump, tad-thump, tad-thump* was heard as they headed up the trail. Elephant Man stopped on his way up the cliff, "This is where I stopped on the way down. There is something about this spot, but there's nothing here except mushrooms."

Coily pushed past Elephant Man. "Yeah, there is something here. A pile of your foul drool from on the way down. Now let's continue up the cliff. There is nothing here to be found."

Cycrabster moved closer to Elephant Man. "I don't see anything either. We should continue to search up farther."

Elephant Man replied, "Okay, it's just a feeling."

Tad-thump, tad-thump, tad-thump was heard as they went up the cliff and back to the split in the path. Elephant Man finally making it back up to the top. "Do you want to go back to Gator with nothing?"

Cycrabster looked around. "We can head toward the castle and see if we missed anything. I don't want to go back empty handed, but we've been gone a while and have found nothing."

Coily looked at the two of them. "There is nothing past the castle or around it. So if we find nothing on the way, maybe they are not here. Maybe they just used this spot of the root system as a stopover for something and that's how they found the children."

Cycrabster responded, "I agree, let's search on our way back to the castle. Then we can let Gator know what we found and what we believe." The three of them once again began to search for the Light Brothers and headed toward the castle. *Tad-thump, tad-thump, tad-thump.*

Chapter 28

Hugo, Birdy, Mush, and his brothers arrived at the castle in no time. Birdy looked around. "This is as close to the gate as Hugo can get without being seen. I will fly up into a tree near Emil. When I see the leaves blow past the gate and close to Emil, I will fly to one of the trees near the river. I will swoop down and then fly toward the children. This way I can be seen and distract the guards."

Hugo looked around. "Okay, we will find three leaves and get prepared." Mush and his brothers searched for the leaves. They each came back with several leaves. Mush looked at Hugo. "You have to do this in one shot. Get all three leaves past the gate and as close to Emil as possible. The rest of the leaves will blow around so that our leaves do not look suspicious. Birdy, is this a straight path to Emil?" Birdy flew overhead and landed on the wall. He came down. "If you go straight that way." He pointed toward the gate and to the right of the wagon but left of the castle. "They will get close to the edge of the castle and around the corner will be Emil," Birdy added.

"Good," replied Hugo. "Now fly to your tree and I will set up all the leaves."

Birdy flew to a tree so that he could see Emil. Emil was still tied up and looked tired. Emil spotted Birdy and winked. Hugo set up three leaves in a row and the other leaves around them. Hugo looked at Mush and his brothers. "Get in your leaves, and I will blow you past the gate and as close to Emil as I can. You can then free him. I will wait in the bushes. Out of sight in case you need help."

Mush and his brothers got positioned in their leaves. Hugo took a deep, deep breath and blew the leaves. Some of the leaves swirled around and blew upward. Others just rolled along the ground. The leaves with the Mush brothers in them rolled through the gate, past the wagon, past the castle walls, and landed at the edge of the castle. This is where they wanted to be, but a guard was near Emil. It was the U Fallen Brother. The Mush brothers stayed in their leaves. The leaves began to unroll, but since they are the Mush brothers, they mushed into the ground under the leaves not to be seen.

Birdy swooped down at the guards and flew toward the river. He then swooped down near the children. They did not look up at him. So Birdy swooped and almost flew into some of the children. They looked and pointed at Birdy. George, remembering what Emil had said about him being rescued, slowly went back toward the castle. Meanwhile, the rest of the children stared at Birdy. The guards took notice of Birdy and the children pointing at the swooping bird. They began to head toward the children. George was now picking fruit at the closest tree to the castle. The guards ran by him, including U.

The Mush brothers all "unmushed" and went to Emil. They used their Mush powers, and Mushy mushed into a key for the lock. Musher mushed into the post and spoke to Emil, "Can you walk? Just nod your head. We are going to go to the gate and morph you with one of us through the gate. Hugo is waiting on the other side to help if you need it. We will go back to the tunnel built by Rooty and the others. You and Shelly will go up the tunnel and go home." Emil shook his head yes. Mush himself still mushed as the ground, looked for other guards.

George made his way to the closest tree and watched Emil. Gator, hearing the commotion, looked upon his kingdom. Gator saw all the guards heading toward the river. He then saw Birdy swooping around the children. Gator summoned, "Guards, guards!" All the guards within the castle approached Gator. Gator commanded, "Go search the grounds around the castle. I fear that our Light Brothers may be close at hand. Go!" All the guards raced out of the castle to search the grounds.

Emil was unchained easily by the Mush brothers. Once free, they all headed for the gate. Emil was not yet strong enough. So Musher mushed into a sled and the other two pulled the sled. Once at the gate, they morphed with Emil through the gate. Then with the help of Hugo, they all retreated into the woods.

George watched as Emil was freed from his chains. George tried to stay close to see what was going to happen next. He was still fearful of the creatures with Emil but decided to stay close. As Emil and the Mush brothers made their way to the gate, George followed. He was not close enough and Emil was on the other side of the gate before George could get there. George hid behind the wagon and watched as Emil, Hugo, and the Mush brothers disappeared into the woods.

Gator, watching from above, saw Birdy fly off past the river's edge and back into the castle grounds and then toward the hidden tunnel. Gator also saw that Emil was not there in the courtyard. Running to the front of the castle, Gator saw nothing. There was no Emil and no Light Brothers. Gator called for his guards, "Guards! Guards! Quick, our prisoner has escaped. I saw the bird flying toward our hidden tunnel. Take a group and go search the tunnel. Send another group to search the grounds of the castle. We need to find the prisoner. And get those children back to work."

As the guards opened the gate and went toward the tunnel, George snuck out and went the other way into the woods to look for Emil. George did not find a path but had watched which way Emil and his friends were heading. George could not see Emil and his friends, but he knew that they were just up ahead. He followed what he thought was a path.

Emil, Hugo, and the Mush brothers were hurrying through the bushes but were being careful in case their Fallen Brothers were on to their trail. They had "unmushed," and Hugo was helping Emil to walk. Birdy met up with Emil, Hugo, and the Mush brothers right near the split in the path. Birdy flew down. "I watched from a nearby bush and a group of our Fallen Brothers headed to their hidden tunnel. And a group stayed inside the gates to search the grounds."

Hugo replied, "We head straight for the tunnel. Tall One and Shelly will be waiting for all of us so Emil can go home." On the way to the tunnel, they explained the rest of the plan to Emil. George could hear talking as he got closer to the split in the path. When George reached the split in the path, there was no one there. He could still hear talking and followed the sounds.

Chapter 29

Cycrabster, Coily, and Elephant Man came out of the tunnel to be greeted by a group of their Fallen Brothers. Cycrabster immediately demanded, "What is doing on?"

The first guard replied, "The prisoner has escaped, and we saw the bird flying toward the tunnel. Did you see anyone?"

Cycrabster grunted. "No one passed us. Let's go back to Gator and let him know what we found or didn't find." The group of Fallen Brothers, Cycrabster, Coily, and Elephant Man, all went back to the castle.

They all met Gator in the dining hall. Cycrabster explained the long journey and the mounds they had found. He explained the steep cliff and how there was nothing else. He also explained their theory that the Light Brothers are not close by but used the root system as a stopover. Gator listened and then spoke angrily and loudly, almost yelling. "Our castle has been infiltrated! Our prisoner has escaped! He is not inside the walls. When we sent all of the children to their bunks, we found that another one was missing!" Everyone was silent. Gator looked around the room. "We must fortify our castle. We must train our bothers better. We must get a better hold of the children.

And we must come up with a plan and find our Light Brothers! And take back what is ours! Our Light Brothers must live nearby to pull off a stunt like this and get past us."

Chapter 30

Emil, Hugo, and the Mush brothers finally reached the tunnel. Rooty, Snailstein, Shelly, and Tall One were waiting outside the tunnel. Shelly ran to Emil and hugged him. "I'm so glad that you are okay." Emil hugged Shelly back.

Tall One looked at the two of them. "We are sad that you two are leaving, but it is what needs to be done. We will try to get the other children and free them. But you two must go now, and we will hide the tunnel." Emil and Shelly thanked everyone, and the two of them, hand in hand, went up the steps of the tunnel to the top. Emil and Shelly pushed through to the top world. They climbed out and found themselves right back where they had started near the river. They were their normal size.

As Emil and Shelly climbed out and stood in the top world, the tunnel collapsed. There was a shaking on the ground and then the earth was as it had been in the top world. There was no sign of a tunnel or even a hint that the earth had been disturbed. Emil and Shelly looked at each other. They both got on their hands and knees trying to find the tunnel, but to no avail.

Emil said, "Let us get you home first. I'm sure everyone is worried." Shelly nodded her head in agreement, and they started toward

Shelly's house. They walked into Shelly's house to find her mother in the kitchen. Shelly's mother turned toward the two children. "Seems like you two have missed lunch again. Emil, I will call your parents and let them know that you will be staying for dinner. Now the two of you, go wash up. Do not disturb your father. The second football game is almost at half time."

Shelly and Emil looked at each other. They had been gone for five days in Lilim, but in their world it was only five hours.

Tall One turned to see a boy come running up. Just then, there was a rumbling around them, and the tunnel collapsed. The tunnel collapsed onto itself and was gone. All that hard work and they didn't even know if Emil and Shelly got home safe. Or what size they were if they had gotten home. George looked at everyone and replied, "My name is George, and I am friends with Emil."

Tall One replied, "It's not safe here. We all need to go back to Lilim." One Arm appeared in front of George. "Welcome to Lilim."

About the Author

Linda has worked with ED youth for over thirty years. She now works with IDD adults. Linda enjoyed writing poetry as a teenager. The inspiration for her book comes from her husband's senior thesis for his BA in fine arts. He created dozens of sculptures of Lilith's children that live in Lilim.